UNEXPECTED EDEN

"If you're a Paranormal Romance lover, I HIGHLY HIGHLY HIGHLY recommend this book. Be warned, you'll be hooked too." – Christina with The Jeep Diva

"It was so easy to fall in love with Lexi and Eryx. I was "willing" them together through every line and ended up entangled in the passion they share and the secrets they were trying to hide from each other." – Jaded with Bitten by Books

"You MAY read this book if you enjoy fantasies; you SHOULD read this book because you are looking for a great romance; but you MUST read this book if you are willing to enter a parallel world full of passion and love!" – More Books Than Livros

"A no muss no fuss, strong debut by a new author that has created a believable world, interesting characters that I actually want to get to know better and a series story arc that I am fully invested in seeing through to its conclusion." – Books-N-Wine

"This was a marvelous story with fun but very sexy characters. I loved the unique world of Morgan's imagination and can't wait to discover more." – Tome Tender

Other Titles

by Rhenna Morgan

WHAT *Janie* WANTS

RHENNA MORGAN

WHAT JANIE WANTS
By Rhenna Morgan

Content Editor – Penny Barber
Copy Editor - Mary Murray
Cover Artwork - The Killion Group, Inc.

ISBN: 151149221X
ISBN-13: 978-1511492218

ACKNOWLDGMENTS

Getting Janie and Zade's story written was truly a whirlwind. I never would have made it through the storm without loads of direction and input from some key individuals. My heartfelt thanks to Jami Denise, T.D. Hart, Sarah Hegger, CJ Burright, Dena Garson, Christina Gwin, and L.J. Anderson for turning things around with zero complaint and answering all those pesky Facebook messages.

Also super big hugs and shout outs to the ladies who whipped my story into the best shape possible—Penny Barber and Mary Murray.

A very special thank you to my wonderful readers. If I didn't have you, writing these stories wouldn't be nearly as fun or rewarding.

As always, my biggest thanks goes to my family. Writing would be empty without your patience, your encouragement and your love.

DEDICATION

To every person who's given tirelessly to others and awakened to find they've lost themselves. I hope you find your colors and paint a masterpiece.

CHAPTER 1

NEVER, EVER TRUST a bohemian minded, globe-trotting sister with travel arrangements. Life advice, maybe. But travel plans? Huh-uh.

Janie shoved her RayBans up for a better look at what had to be the Riviera Maya's last remaining seventies throwback. Turquoise stucco walls, check. Architecture à la Frank Lloyd Wright, check. Cheesy marquee styled like the Gilligan's Island logo—check, check, check.

Gypsy Cove.

It sounded like a place Emmy would pick. Tiny, quirky, and way, way off the beaten path. The odds of finding any cute little thatched roof huts or designer pools overlooking the ocean like she'd seen online were slim, but they probably had a whole storeroom full of little umbrellas for the drinks.

Behind her, the taxi driver sped out of the cobblestone circular drive, dousing Janie in a puff of lung-choking exhaust. Apropos of her life, lately. One fast getaway and a big old mess left behind.

She waved the smoke off and lumbered toward the unattended bell stand, her purse, overnight tote, and rolling suitcase vying for the chance to whop her off balance. The halter-top linen jumper she'd bought as a part of her suddenly single vacation wardrobe hugged her full figure a little tighter than it had the mannequin, but at least it was cool. August temps in Mexico could give hell a run for its money.

Surely they'd have a spa. Or at least a massage therapist. Wasn't that a Caribbean requirement? Though, with the looks of this place, she'd probably get a masseur with long hair named Stoney instead of a muscled up man in a polo and golf shorts.

"Oh, there you are." A wiry middle-aged man with dull brown, thinning hair that stuck out in all directions and a much thicker mustache, loped down the short steps, flip-flops slapping with each stride. The poor guy's tropical shirt was as wrinkled as Janie felt. "Dahlia said you'd be here. Janie McAlister, right?"

"Yes, I'm Janie. How did you know it was me? Who's Dahlia?"

He oomphed and hefted her overstuffed suitcase up the stairs in an awkward arch that would have thrown her back out for days. "Dahlia's my wife. We own the place. She kicked me out of beach bingo to check you in. Also said to give you the room closest to the point 'cause you had shit to work through."

She'd never met a Dahlia in her life, let alone made travel arrangements with one.

Emmy. Her well-intentioned but meddlesome sister knew all kinds of strange and oddly wonderful people. Janie could all too easily picture her sister on the phone plotting ways to pull her out of her post-divorce funk. Shit to work through indeed. "I'm sorry. I'm afraid you've got me at a bit of a loss."

He plunked the suitcase down in front of the luau knock-off reception desk and darted to the computer on the other side. Pointy-fingering the keyboard about as fast as Janie texted on her new iPhone, he wrinkled his nose and squinted at the screen. His voice reminded her of Kramer on Seinfeld. "Most people are at a loss with my Dahlia. People with the gift are a little intimidating at first, but you learn to roll with it after a while."

"People with the gift?"

"The gift." He yanked a cabinet door open and a whole panel of old-fashioned keys with lacquered wood key fobs clanked against the surface. "The Sight. Premonitions. Connected to the universe." He plucked one key off its hook and slammed the door shut. "The kind of mystical intel you don't ignore."

Yep, she was gonna kill Emmy.

"Now, I've got you in the Dreamweaver suite. It's one of the best." He shuffled from behind his desk and handed over the key and a folder full of resort information then pointed toward a hallway at the far side of the lobby. "Head that way 'till you run out of doors. Yours is the last one. Perfect view of the beach. We'll keep the mini-bar in your room stocked, but better stuff is at the poolside bar. The kitchen is at the center of the complex. Meal times are posted in the info pack in your room, but there are healthy snacks available twenty-four hours a day. All organic and locally grown foods, of course. I'll bring your suitcase as soon as I wrap up here."

Well, that didn't sound too bad. The style of the place might be outdated, but the lobby was clean and cozy. Plenty of sitting areas and potted palms with coral flowers nestled between them for privacy. Maybe she'd skip murdering her sister and settle for good old-fashioned torture. She offered her hand. "Thanks for getting me settled, Mr....?"

"Oh." He smacked himself on the forehead and shook her hand. "Silly me. I'm Arlo."

A hippie professor. Arlo reminded her of Donald Sutherland back in his *Animal House* days, complete with

3

twinkling, pale blue eyes and crooked smile. Happiness fairly rolled off him, buffeting a good chunk of her travel tension.

"It's nice to meet you, Arlo. Your resort is lovely." In a retro kind of way. "I'm sure it'll be everything my sister promised."

"We always get exactly what we need when we need it. The trick is grabbing onto it when it comes spinning around."

Hmmm. Definitely friends of Emmy. Same advice, different location. Trouble was, it was hard to glom on to a life preserver when your world was spinning like a cyclone down the drain.

"Now, off you go." He waved her toward the hallway. "Spend a little time getting familiar with your room and kick your feet up. You need anything at all, just let me know and we'll get you taken care of."

After four and a half hours of airports, taxis, and juggling luggage, a little quiet downtime wouldn't hurt. She could tackle Gypsy Cove and its seventies flashback with a whole new, healthy perspective later. She smiled and waggled a playful goodbye. "I think you give good advice, Arlo. Take your time with the luggage."

Feet up. Relaxing. Air-conditioning. Maybe after a nap she'd call Emmy and get to the bottom of Arlo and the mysterious Dahlia.

She dropped her room key in her purse, flipped open the resort info packet, and strolled toward the hallway. Food and drinks available twenty-four hours a day. One pool at the center of the resort. One reserved beachfront cabana (*palapa*) per room, per day. Non-motorized water sports available on request. Beaches, clothing optional.

Janie froze and yanked the amenities flier free of the folder.

Beaches, clothing optional.

No way. No. Freaking. Way. Emmy had lost her damned mind.

Janie closed her eyes and sucked in a deep, calming breath. Nothing to freak out about. She'd just find another, more mainstream place to stay until she could rebook her flight home. Back to what she knew. Back to where it was safe.

See? Problem solved. Easy peasy.

And then she'd kill her sister.

She snapped the folder shut, spun around for the front desk, and slammed into a wall of hard, delicious man.

Zade fumbled the football Devin had thrown him, gripped the up close and personal redhead by both shoulders, and tried to keep them from falling.

Her tote swung out. She over-corrected, and gravity took over.

Zade tucked her up tight and spun into the fall. His shoulder slammed into the unfinished stone floors and her knee hit him square in the nuts.

"Fuck." He rolled to his side and held on for dear life to the soft body pressed against him. Blue and white flashes fired bigger than a Dallas Fourth of July show behind his clenched eyelids. His stomach knotted and his lungs flat out stopped.

"Oh." The woman jerked in his hold. "Oh, my God. Did I just…" She wiggled more and broke from his grip. "Oh, my God, I did. Shoot."

Small but firm hands pressed against his shoulder, like she was trying to keep him in place. Did she think he was gonna hop up and go somewhere?

"I'm so sorry," she said. "Just take nice slow breaths."

Too much talking. Waaay too much talking. Christ, was that Devin laughing in the background? He counted to ten and tried to pull in a breath, a wave of nausea bubbling up from his gut. He couldn't go into fetal position. Not with an audience. Especially Devin.

Quick footsteps slapped against the tile. More voices echoed through the lobby, urgent, but quieter.

The roiling in his belly calmed a bit, replaced with a sting that radiated up from his groin.

Comforting fingers smoothed his bangs out of his eyes and stroked his forehead. "Maybe you should get him some ice?"

"No." The grunt-gurgle combo was the best he could manage, but at least no one would get near his 'nads with an icepack.

"Wow, Dahlia said this was gonna be a funny one to watch. I think I'm gonna have to help her understand what men consider funny."

Arlo. Thank God. "What's Dahlia got to do with my nuts taking an unexpected trip north?"

"I'm so sorry," the redhead said. "I wasn't paying attention."

"S'all good." He waved toward her voice and focused on not cupping his sac. "You looked like you were in a hurry. Go. Let Arlo take care of what you needed. I'm gonna need a minute to unwind my eyeballs from the back of my head."

"Devin," Arlo said as he urged Zade up from the floor, "head back down to the beach and take the football with you. Was there something wrong, Ms. McAllister?"

Ms. McAllister? Kinda formal for Uncle Arlo. Zade sat up and rested his arms on his knees, giving his boys plenty of wiggle room.

"Um." Bags shifted and papers rustled. "Why don't you see to the young man first? I can...I'll wait until you get a minute."

Arlo slapped Zade on the shoulder and stood between Zade and the antsy Ms. McAllister. "A few more minutes and he'll be all suave and swagger again." Arlo shifted beside him, flip-flops squeaking on the hard floor. "Well, maybe not as much swagger today, but he'll be fine. Probably best we give him a minute. So? What is it you need?"

6

Zade rolled his head and let out a slow breath. Mind over matter. All he needed to do was open his eyes, stand, and hobble back to his room where he could groan in private.

"I hate to inconvenience you," she said, "but I think there's been a mistake. I was hoping you could call me a taxi."

Damn, Ms. McAllister had a rockin' voice. All husky and breathless. Zade pried his eyes open and got an eyeful of his uncle's scrawny backside.

"A mistake?" Arlo said. "What kind of mistake? The Dreamweaver suite is the best one we have. Well, aside from the Stargazer bungalow, but it's occupied."

"I'm sure the room is lovely. It's just that…" Ms. McAlister shifted and held something out in front of Arlo. Long wavy auburn hair spilled down her back, lots of wild and sexy layers. The tropical outfit she had on would have come off asinine on one of the twiggy chicks down on the beach, but on her it looked sultry. "…and I'm not sure that's appropriate for me."

Whoa. Helluva bad time to tune out on a conversation. Zade cleared his throat. "What's not appropriate?"

Arlo spun and faced him, giving him a full view of the woman who'd played defensive line with his nuts.

Well, hello, Ms. McAllister.

The hair and body weren't the only thing she had working for her. Hell, her quirky, full-lipped smile alone was enough to make him push his shoulders back and muscle through the lingering burn. No way was he sitting on his ass another second. He pushed himself up and prayed his legs would keep him vertical.

"Ms. McAlister's a little uncomfortable with our beach policy," Arlo said.

She hugged the folder to her chest. "Not with the policy. I think it's a wonderful option to offer your guests. I'm just afraid I won't fit in."

Ah, that policy. Funny. With her curves, he'd give half the

money he'd earned selling his business to see her au naturale on the beach. He eased forward and fought back a wince. "Hey, Arlo. Why don't you give me and your guest a minute to talk?"

"Shouldn't you sit down for a bit?" she said. "I mean, my son had an accident on the football field a few seasons back and he was a little bungled up for a day or so."

Arlo lowered his voice. "Zade, are you sure—"

"I'm good. If Ms. McAllister still wants to go after we talk, I'll drive her over to the Paradisus."

Arlo shuffled off, shaking his head.

"I can take a taxi." She gestured toward his hips then snatched her hand back and covered her mouth. "You should sit. Or lie down, or something."

"Pretty sure my manhood would bounce back a lot faster if the sexy woman who took me down a notch would unpack her bags and not high-tail it for a cookie cutter resort."

She dropped her hand and glanced over her shoulder. Then over to Arlo at the check-in desk. Then down the empty hallway where the nicer suites waited. "Me?"

Damn. He'd seen a lot of women unaware of their impact on men, but he wouldn't have tapped this lady as one. "There's one Homo sapiens without a penis in this lobby and it's been years since I had an imaginary girlfriend."

A delicate pink crawled up her neck and she ducked her chin. "That's sweet of you. I'm really sorry for the accident."

Man, he loved how redheads blushed. Though he'd be able to appreciate the color a whole lot more if she relaxed enough to unwind the death grip on her purse and actually looked at him for more than two seconds. "You're not the first forceful object who's had a run-in with my junk. Doubt you'll be the last. You could make it up to me, though."

"What?

Finally. Eye contact. And they were stellar. Hazel and bright. Big and capped with naturally curved screen goddess eyebrows. She could probably put a man in his place just by

8

lifting one and frowning if she wanted to.

"You could unpack." He jerked his head toward Arlo at the check in desk. "My uncle seemed pretty intent on you staying here." Not that he'd share the whys behind Arlo wanting her to stay put. No man wanted to put his heart and soul into a business only to face make-or-break in the slow season.

She studied Arlo a second and the tension in her shoulders loosened. "He's your family?"

"Yep. He and Aunt Dahlia are good people."

"Do you work here too?"

"Me?" Zade jammed his hands into his swim trunk pockets and shifted to ease the ache between his legs. "Nah. I come about once a year. Usually in the winter, but needed a place to do a little regrouping. Gypsy Cove's good for that."

"Yes, well." She stared at the beach in the distance. "I'm not so sure I'd be as comfortable regrouping here."

"You mean the clothing optional thing."

She opened her mouth, shut it, straightened up nice and tall, and started again. "That's exactly what I mean."

Spunk to go with the rest of the package. Definitely a perk. Hell, to his mind, attitude was the best part of a woman. With the keen attention aimed his way right now, he'd be willing to bet she had a ton of it buried beneath those polite manners.

"You know, only about a quarter of the guests actually take advantage of the policy, and even then it's usually on a dare." He indulged in a good long, up and down of her full figure. "And you don't give yourself enough credit. You'd look perfect naked on the beach."

Her jaw dropped.

"Don't look so shocked. You've got a fantastic body." He offered his hand and winked. "My name's Zade, by the way. Zade Painel."

"Janie McAllister." She shook his hand, but he was pretty sure it was reflexive good manners more than purposeful intent. "You're a direct young man."

Ouch. Direct he could take as a compliment, but the *young man* stung. He rubbed his sternum and quieted his mind. The answers always came when he needed them if he took the time to stop and listen. "Young, maybe. But a professional, nonetheless." Yep, the answers always came. "I've been photographing women for seven years and made a good living doing it. I know sexy when I see it."

She jerked back and blinked several times. "Well, I... Thank you."

"You're welcome. Now are you going to head to the Dreamweaver suite and take advantage of the only private cove in Playa del Carmen? Or are you going to let a pesky clothing detail herd you into one of the vanilla resorts?"

Her lips pressed into a tight line, but twitched at one corner. She huffed out a resigned-sounding breath. "Seeing as how your manhood is at stake, and you've so graciously outlined the benefits of this resort, it seems I'd be foolish not to give it a try."

"Excellent. Then say you'll meet me at the pool for your first cocktail too."

"I think that's pushing it." Yep. The one-raised-eyebrow glare was a killer.

No ring on her finger, so that was promising. He'd still have to get past the young man thing. Kinda made him feel like he should be in knee breeches. "Just offering you the benefit of a well-seasoned traveler in Mexico."

She smirked and hefted her bags higher on each shoulder. "Your uncle's right. Your swagger might be wounded, but your suave is just fine." She glanced at Arlo bustling behind the check-in desk. "You'll let him know?"

"Anything for a valued guest." He motioned down the empty hallway. "Go get settled. Read the rest of the stuff in the folder and let me know if you see something you want to do. I'm usually around." He waggled his eyebrows. "Sometimes I'm at the beach, though."

"Ugh." She tapped him on the shoulder and cast an exasperated scowl at him as she took off down the hall. "Suave indeed."

God he'd missed that. Giving a beautiful woman who didn't realize she was beautiful a different lens to see herself through. Hands down, it had been the best part of his work. And then he'd gone and screwed it up.

He hobbled to Arlo and the new set of guests gathered round the registration desk. He'd figure out what to do with his business. That's what he'd come here for. And while he was at it, he'd spend a little extra time making sure Janie McAlister saw how amazing she was.

CHAPTER 2

NON-COMPETE COVENANT. *For a period of two years after the effective date of this Agreement, Zade Painel will not directly or indirectly engage in any business that competes with Boudoir International. This covenant shall apply to the geographical area that includes the state of Texas.*

Damned legalese. Zade flipped the page on the contract hard enough, it nearly ripped free of the staple at the corner.

"You're looking too hard." Arlo set a neon yellow tumbler full of fresh-squeezed orange juice in front of Zade and swiped a worn dishrag across the bar. "Dahlia told you you'd find the answer when it was time. And what are you doing up this early, anyway? You never leave the bungalow before eleven."

With the shade of the thatched poolside bar and the steady ocean breeze, the mid-morning climate wasn't bad. Under Mexico's direct sun in August, anything past nine was a challenge. "I was inspired to catch the sunrise?"

Arlo huffed and hunkered over his daily inventory clipboard. "More like angling for another round with Ms. McAlister."

"Since when do you use last names with the guests? Her name's Janie."

"Janie, is it?"

Zade laughed and chucked a wadded up cocktail napkin at his uncle. "If you knew what got me up so early, why'd you ask?"

"Got you out of scowling at your contract, didn't it?"

Well, hell. For a scrawny guy without a lick of experience with kids, Arlo was a pretty sly dude. "So, did she show for breakfast?"

Arlo lifted his head only enough to meet Zade's gaze from under his sternly pinched eyebrows. "You should watch yourself with her. Your aunt says she's been through a rough time and came here to find herself, not end up twisted into knots by a camera slinging Don Juan."

"Yeah, well, I'm not slinging my camera anymore, am I?" Not for a period of two years in the state of Texas, which was mighty inconvenient since that was precisely where he lived. God, he'd been an idiot to ink that deal. Or, more accurately, to believe the people he'd sold his business to would carry on with what he'd started the way they were supposed to. "And just because I photographed them in their bedroom doesn't make me a Don Juan."

"No, but I'll swear you came out of the womb seducing women. Must've gotten extra pheromones or something because the nurses couldn't keep their hands off you. I thought your dad and I were going to have to restrain your mother to keep her from killing a few of them who tried to hog you for themselves."

Zade shrugged and sipped his O.J. "Yeah, well, if I've got something special, it doesn't work on all of them."

Arlo straightened from his list and waggled his pencil. "So, that's it."

"What's it?"

"Janie."

"What about her?"

Arlo grinned and ran this thumb through his mustache. "She shut you down."

Hell, yes, she had. The term "young man" had ping-ponged around in his head for way too long last night, though he'd short-circuited the bad juju with a wicked fantasy of a certain redhead and a white-knuckled orgasm that had left him light headed.

"I'm glad." Arlo yanked open the stainless steel bar fridge and scanned the contents. "A challenge is just what you need to forget about that whole business deal. If you can unwind a little, you'll find a solution. But remember what I said about Janie's situation."

Women shrieked and loud splashes sounded from the pool. Four women fussed and swiped water off their perfectly oiled bodies as their male counterparts surfaced from the churning water. At the center of the cannon-ball brigade, a lanky dark-haired man shook his head like a dog and splattered a woman perched on the pool's edge who gave another ear-splitting shout.

Devin and his college entourage. They were nice enough and came in handy for beach sports, but acted closer to twelve than twenty-two. How they'd managed to coordinate, book, and travel together without getting lost was purely a miracle.

Janie probably had him lumped in the same category. A challenge, indeed.

The men's guffaws trailed off and a few of them straightened to their full height, shoulders pushed back. Every eye was aimed opposite their slim and trim cheering section.

Janie.

Damn. No wonder Devin's posse had puffed up and thrown down their best caveman poses. Unlike the neon string bikini-clad women poolside, Janie wore an ivory one-piece. Classy, and though simple, it emphasized her killer curves and lifted her generous breasts up for male exaltation. With a see-through matching sarong draped around her hips and her hair piled on top of her head, she was an outrageously fuckable work of art.

She sashayed around the chaotic college crew and aimed toward the quieter side of the pool in full sun. Adjusting her movie star sunglasses, she scanned the lounge chairs.

Nope. None available that wouldn't put her smack between other guests. Great when you were up for meeting new people, not so much if you were after peace and quiet. Considering the death grip she had on her beach bag, he'd bet conversation wasn't on the agenda.

She paused, surveyed the pool's perimeter, and re-directed herself to the towel cabana off to one side.

Oh, hell. He'd appreciated her perky ass yesterday, but paired with her softly tanned thighs today, he wanted to do a whole lot more than appreciate. More like bend her over, stroke the back of her thighs and—

"What's she doing?" Arlo's voice slashed through his fantasy.

Towel tucked under one arm, Janie meandered through the shade of the tall palm trees lining the far edge of the pool area, this time checking the rowdier side for any isolated loungers.

Zade shifted on his barstool and adjusted his semi-aroused dick. "Not sure I care, as long as she keeps walking."

She moseyed to one lone chair near the pool steps and began unloading her bag.

A fat spray of water arced from the pool's surface and sliced across Janie's shoulder. She shot upright, the *O* shape of her mouth a testament to the water's coldness.

The girl who'd inadvertently splashed Janie jumped on her boyfriend's back and shouted over one shoulder, "Sorry!"

Janie waved the apology off and cast the girl an

understanding smile. "Not a problem."

The hell, it wasn't. She'd already tucked her bag back in place and backed away from the lounger.

"They're going to run her off." Arlo tossed his rag down and hustled from behind the bar. "I knew better than to run a college special. They're all wrong for our resort."

"Hold up." Zade hopped down from his stool and motioned his uncle back behind the bar. "Three more days, and they're gone. They're filling what, half the rooms? That's enough to keep your staff paid up through high season."

"It won't matter, if they ruin the experience for potential return customers."

Janie ambled away from the pool down the wide stamped concrete path toward the lobby. The woman had perfect hips. Made for a man's touch and attention.

Zade clamped a hand on Arlo's shoulder and winked. "Well, then. I'll go see if I can't compensate any discomfort Ms. McAlister might be feeling with a little one on one personalized experience."

Nine in the morning and less than an hour from a shower, and Janie already felt wilted. God, Mexico in August was hot. Emmy wasn't just insane. She was a sadist.

A young couple exited the shadowed lobby hand in hand. The girl's swimsuit barely varied from those at the pool, although the mango color sure worked a lot better than the blatant neon selections the others had worn. It was like they all went to the same stylist—string bikini, beach blond hair, and belly button ring. As soon as she got home, she and her daughter, Mckenna, were going to have a nice long reminder talk about the importance of self-image.

The couple padded closer.

Oh, to be that thin again. Without wrinkles and defiant of

gravity. Janie sucked in her gut and squared her shoulders. She'd thought the few trips to the tanning bed would take the edge off her fair, redhead skin tone, but under the vicious Mexico sun, she looked as white as ever. The ivory swimsuit wasn't helping. Maybe the girls were right to go with bolder colors.

The couple passed with a twin set of curious smiles.

A few more steps and the lobby's shade engulfed her, easing the sun's powerful bite on her shoulders. She should've found a lounger in the shade. Surely her mini-tan could peek through there, not to mention camouflage some of her cellulite. A total win-win. Better, if she'd had a good night's sleep to go with it. Her room was lovely, with lots of bold, beautiful colors and a bed twice as comfy as her ten-year-old king-size back home, but she'd stayed up way too long tossing and turning over the man she'd inadvertently groped and kneed the day before.

Zade Painel. What a name. Though, it fit him.

God, she should be ashamed. He couldn't be more than a few years older than her son, Thomas. But the way he'd considered her, so focused and interested in every little detail, despite what she'd done to him. And the feel of his warm skin, how solid he'd been, pressed next to her.

Nope. No. No. No. Not a direction her thoughts needed to take.

She snatched a flier off the brochure rack. Time to make the most out of what life had given her. Or, as she coached her kids, reassess and revise.

Tulum and Jungle Maya With Ziplines and Rappelling.

Ugh. In August? She'd be soaked in sweat before she ever got off the tour bus. Although, Thomas would get a kick out of the ziplines and rappelling.

Swim With The Dolphins.

Oh, now that would be fun, but kind of awkward alone. Still, who would know? It would be like eating out or going to a movie solo. No big deal. As of last week, she was officially forty. Surely she could swing a little one-on-one time with some dolphins.

All Inclusive Catamaran to Isla Mujeres.

Well, that sounded lovely. Wind, food, and drink. Probably peaceful, too. Hard to fit half a resort full of college age kids on a catamaran.

"Not a fan of the *Animal House* crowd, huh?"

Oh, boy. Zade. She'd hoped she wouldn't have to come face to face with him again during her trip. Sort of. The dirty thoughts her mind had put front and center last night didn't count.

She flipped the catamaran brochure over, kept her back to him, and scrambled for an exit strategy. "What makes you think that?"

"Well, after you circled the pool a few times, I figured it wasn't too likely you'd come in for a landing."

Damn. So much for looking blasé about the whole thing.

"You know, every suite has a *palapa* reserved on the beach," he said.

"I thought I'd work my way up to the beach."

"Ah. Clothing optional. I forgot." The way he chuckled at the last little bit said he hadn't, but thought it was cute. He motioned at the tall brochure stand. "I can recommend a few, if you want. Or better yet, take you on a custom one."

"I appreciate the offer, but I'm sure you have better things to do with your day than cart an out of place woman around Mexico."

"Actually, you're not the one out of place. Arlo usually pulls in crowds over thirty, but he thought he'd try a few August specials on college campuses. Between the noise complaints and the room damage, I'm pretty sure he'll never do that again." He paused and shifted directly into her line of sight. "You know, the *palapa* for your room is more isolated than the rest. Why don't you let me show you where it is? I'll run interference if we come across any skin-loving free spirits on the way."

For a man close to Thomas' age, they sure talked differently. Everything out of Thomas' mouth tended to end with a goofy ha-ha or snort. Zade sounded…well, older.

She chanced a peek up from her brochure.

Yep, bare chested again. Black board shorts and barefoot. She didn't dare look into those blue eyes of his again. They'd kept her up long enough last night as it was.

Ugh. Divorced three months, and she was already turning into a pervy old woman.

"Come on." He dipped his knees until he was in her line of sight, which only emphasized how tall he was compared to her. "What's the worst that could happen? You're a grown woman on a quiet vacation in paradise. Live a little."

Her ex, Gerald, had certainly lived a little. So what, if she let a handsome man almost half her age keep her company? There couldn't be more than fifty rooms total in this resort, and half of them were filled with people who wouldn't so much as register her existence, let alone rush home to alert the media.

She tucked her brochures in her bag and lifted her chin. "You're absolutely right." Reassess and Revise. "It's not like I've never seen a naked body before, and a run-in might make for a good story when I get home."

"That's the spirit." His eyes twinkled with way too much knowledge and a punch of mischief that stole her breath. He turned her with a hand at her elbow and guided her down the hallway toward her suite. "So, tell me what brings you to Gypsy Cove."

Surely he wasn't expecting to go to her room. "Um, my sister Emmy. The trip was a gift."

"Nice gift. Has she been here before?"

"I have no idea." Though she intended to get the details from her sister as soon as she could set up a Skype session this afternoon. Talking to Emmy before noon was a bad idea all around. "She acted like it was the perfect place for me to figure things out, so my guess is yes. Though with Emmy, there's no telling."

"What is it you need to figure out?"

Oops. Probably not the best line of conversation for a young guy with a devilish gleam in his eye. Where were they headed? "Just next steps. Life choices."

"Sounds mysterious." He paced beside her, their steps drawing them closer and closer to her room. He had such a breathtaking build. Not overly muscular, but not lanky either. His blond hair reached his jawline in a kind of man-bob, short enough to be respectable, long enough to be rebellious. "You know, my mom says when the universe wants you in a particular place, or to learn a particular lesson, it keeps after you until you learn what it needs you to see. The best you can do is delay the learning, not put it off entirely."

The end of the hallway loomed with nothing but suite entrances on every side. "Your mom sounds very wise."

"She's one of the most amazing women on the planet." He stopped beside her door and held out his hand for the key. "Something tells me you're pretty amazing too."

CHAPTER 3

ZADE FOUGHT LIKE hell not to laugh at the terrified expression on Janie's face. She zigzagged her attention between him and the door so many times it was a wonder she didn't strain her neck.

He waggled his fingers as a reminder he was waiting for the key. "Relax, Janie. It's just a shortcut to your *palapa*."

"Oh." Blinking, she blushed as prettily as she had yesterday, and rummaged in her bag. "You threw me for a second."

"Not to worry. I'm not out to ravage you." He took the key, opened the door, and winked over his shoulder. "Yet."

Man, this woman was priceless. Effortlessly beautiful and full of expression. He'd love to have an hour alone with her and a camera. To capture the way she quirked her mouth, that sweet blush, and the way she looked as she lowered her eyelids over an expression heavy with need.

Splaying his hand at the small of her back, he urged her forward, and barely stifled the need to palm the curve of her ass. "From your patio, the *palapa* isn't far."

She hurried forward and glanced back at the point of contact. "You said you normally visit your uncle in winter," she said, more breathless than before. "Why the change?"

Hell, if she had any idea how active his imagination was at the moment, she'd sprint straight out the sliding glass door and all the way to Isla Mujera. He ushered her outside and across the open patio. "Ah, so you're not willing to share your secrets, but you want mine."

Janie's eyes popped wide. "I didn't mean to pry."

He motioned toward the circular thatched shelters near the beach, pocketed his hands in his board shorts, and trailed behind her. It was either that, or cup the back of her neck and see if her skin was as smooth as it looked. "I've got no problem sharing. I made a bad business call and I can't figure out how to fix it. The whole thing's got me off center, so I came here to regroup."

She stopped at the closest *palapa* and stared with the same slack-jawed wonder everyone else got with their first look at Gypsy Cove. Still aqua water and pristine, powder-white sand. The one peaceful taste of heaven on Playa del Carmen's otherwise buffeted shores. And at this time of day, most guests were more interested in food than sun, so the cove was pretty deserted.

Zade ambled closer, grateful for the time to openly appreciate the far more appealing view Janie created while she studied the beach. "This one's yours. You want sun or shade?"

Janie craned her neck toward the sun and shielded her eyes. "It's probably a horrid idea with my skin, but I think I'd like to try to get some sun."

"Can't have you go home without a tan." Zade pulled one of the two cushioned loungers out of the shade and angled it so she'd get an even tan. He tugged the second one alongside it. "You mind if I hang with you for a bit? All the noise at the pool rakes at me after awhile. Plus, I figure having someone around to fight off the streakers might not be a bad plan. At least, until you decide you're ready for commando."

She placed her bag and book on the small table, and grinned up at him. "That's not happening. Not here. Not ever. I'm too old for that."

"We'll see." He stretched out and closed his eyes.

Janie's room key jingled and clanked against something plastic as she rummaged through her bag. "So, what's the bad business decision?"

He rolled his shoulders and stretched his neck to ease the quick pressure spike at the base of his neck. Every time the topic came up, it reminded him of how gullible he'd been, and it rankled deep. Still, Janie was talking. And if she was talking, then they had a chance of moving on to other, more interesting topics. Or doing. Doing would be good. "I sold my business to some people who said they'd do one thing with it and ended up doing something else."

Janie settled on the lounger beside him. "You sold a business?"

He pried open one eye and twisted his head for a better view of her.

She popped the lid on a neon orange bottle of sport-strength suntan lotion and shook out a palmfull. "I can't even get my son to think about work, let alone have a business to consider selling."

"How old's your son?"

"Twenty-one."

"God, is he even out of college yet?"

"No, but I'd like him to think about being self-supporting one of these days. He's only got a year before graduation, and I'm not convinced he knows what he's going to do after."

"Maybe he doesn't."

"Sounds like you did."

Hell, yes, he did. With a camera, he could capture things other people missed. Making women the central focus of his lens was a perk. He closed his eyes. Alternative music drifted over from the pool, but it was quiet enough not to drown out the surf. The cove was always peaceful, but something about Janie's presence made it more so. "I loved what I did."

"Why'd you sell it, then?"

"Stupid." The burn that billowed up every time he thought about what he'd done cranked into high gear, and he rubbed his chest above his heart. "They offered me a sweet deal on a buyout, and promised me they'd stick to the same plan and principle I'd started it on."

The steady swish as Janie rubbed lotion into her legs sounded next to him. A coconut scent carried right behind it. "You said you're a photographer, right?"

That made two details she'd remembered about him. Either she had an exceptional memory, or Ms. McAlister had given him a thought or two since yesterday. "Yep."

"So, how could they screw that up?"

Well, this would be interesting. He sat up, planted his feet in the sand, and rested his elbows on his knees. "Because I had a specialty business. One that catered to women. One I busted my balls to make sure came across as tasteful and made them feel good about themselves."

"What kind of specialty?"

He smiled, poised to catch her reaction as if he had his camera. "Boudoir shots."

Janie's hand froze mid forearm and she snapped her head around so hard, a strand of auburn hair tumbled over one eye. "Boudoir?"

"Nothing trashy," he said. "All tasteful and meant to draw out a woman's beauty. Usually with the help of their partner or husband."

She licked her lip and started back up with the lotion, moving up to her shoulders in slower, deeper strokes. Shifting to face front, she focused on her toes and acted like they were chatting up the weather. In a tone a notch lower, she said, "And they screwed it up how?"

"You familiar with Glamour Shots?"

Her sharp laugh rang out across the cove and ricocheted back to them. Her easy smile stretched ear-to-ear, all the awkwardness of seconds ago obliterated. "Oh, Lord. Please tell me they didn't gaudy up something good?"

"Double gaudy. Cheesy corsets, stilettos, and Photoshop. Everything that flies in the face of what I wanted to give them."

"Give who?"

"Women."

Janie's gaze locked with his and, for a second, he wondered if she was holding her breath. She rolled her lips inward the way women did when trying to smooth out their lipstick, twisted as though looking for something behind her, and flicked the bottle's top closed.

Her back. She couldn't reach her back with the lotion. The cut of the swimsuit was low and her barely tanned skin was on display. Talk about divine intervention.

He stood and tugged the bottle from her grip. "Scoot up."

"Huh?"

"Scoot up."

Warily, she studied him.

He straddled the lounger behind her and sat.

"What are you doing?"

He squeezed out enough lotion to make damned sure he'd have to rub for a while. "Helping you with your sunscreen."

"You can't do that."

"Why not? Would you rather burn?"

Janie twisted. "But it's not appropri—"

His hands connected on either side of her spine and her shoulders snapped back. "Easy," he murmured, curling his thumbs and kneading the back of her neck. "Just relax."

Bit by bit, her muscles unclenched and her breathing grew choppy.

God, what was it about this woman? Touching her felt like more than just physical contact. There was a foundation to it. A soul-deep connection and communication that made

25

every other intimate moment he'd had with other women seem cheap in comparison.

She let her head fall forward, and a few loose tendrils fell forward with it. A moan of satisfaction vibrated beneath his palm.

Slow and easy, he worked the lotion into her smooth skin. Relaxed movements meant to sooth and entice. He nudged her shoulder straps a little wider apart, and dipped his fingertips under them. "When's the last time someone touched you, Janie?"

The pool noise faded to nothing, but the soft, peaceful pattern of wind, waves, and birds seemed to thicken and amplify.

A tiny shiver shook her. "A long time."

God, he'd like to fix that. Knock those damned swimsuit straps aside and cup her breasts. He'd bet anything she'd be twice as responsive sexually as she was when talking with him. "Humans weren't meant to be without contact. Touch can cure things words can't even get close to."

She peered at him over her shoulder. "Sometimes you say the most mature things."

One step past young man, at least. Probably best not to rush it, though. He liked the feel of her beneath his hands too much, all pliant and loose. No way was he screwing this up.

"Why boudoir shots?" she asked.

He dragged his fingers up the sides of her torso, not so far as to touch the sides of her breasts, but enough to hint. "Because women are beautiful. Perfect creatures. Because there's nothing more powerful than when they gift someone with their intimacy. I wanted to capture it. To help every client find their own unique beauty and save it for them so they could see it later."

She twisted. "And they made it ugly."

He dropped his hands. "And they made it ugly."

He stood, set the lotion on the table, and stretched out on

his chair.

"Thank you." Her voice barely registered against the water and the wind, but it was still enough to make his dick swell and take note. All raspy, low, and decadent. "That was nice."

"You seem surprised."

"No. Yes. I mean…" She wiggled and gripped the armrest. "It's inappropriate. I'm too old for you."

Damn. Back to that again. "No you're not."

"You don't even know how old we're talking about."

"It wouldn't matter if I did. Age is a number. You're a person. I find a lot about you attractive, and when a man finds a woman who appeals to him on many levels, he generally tries to find a way to get his hands on her."

"I don't think you understand." She splayed her arms wide. "I'm forty. As in, old enough to be your mother."

Zade closed his eyes and centered his head again. "My mom's a pretty rockin' chick. I've seen her turn heads from twenty to sixty, and the ones she takes home are the ones who click with her, not the ones who fall into an appropriate age group."

"Where's your dad?"

Zade fisted his hand to keep from rubbing his chest. "Dead. Died when I was a teenager. Cancer. But she didn't die with him. She mourned, pulled herself up, and taught me to live life."

"I'm sorry."

So sensitive. He liked that about her. How she seemed to tread carefully even around strangers. "Don't be. I loved my dad and he loved us. It was just his time. We live while we're here, then we move on."

Quiet stretched between them. Dahlia's meditation chime sounded from the pier around the bend, and a seagull chirped overhead.

"My son is twenty-one," she said.

"So you mentioned."

Zade paced his breaths and concentrated on the sun's warmth along his skin.

"You can't be much older than him," she said.

So, that was it. He sat upright and faced her, a grin he knew he should hide, but couldn't quite manage to stop, whipping into place. "You're not gonna let this age thing go, are you?"

Janie frowned at the horizon for a few heartbeats, then slid her gaze to him. So much desire there, but pain too. Conflict. "When I look at you I can't help but think about my son."

"When I touched you, were you thinking about your son?"

"No." Breathless. A husky tone he wanted to hear behind all kinds of other phrases. Preferably, *"Yes."*

"That's because I'm not," he said. "I'm a man interested in a woman. Interested in getting to know you. Interested in finding all the best ways to touch you and make you sigh the way you did five minutes ago. And if I'm lucky, seeing the look on your face when you come."

Janie sputtered as if he'd tossed a bucket full of ice water square in her face. "You can't be serious."

"Why the hell not?"

"I'm forty ye—"

"Besides age."

She opened her mouth to speak, then closed it.

"It was your eyes that got me first," he said. "Not the color, but the way you looked at me. The way you made contact and made me feel like I was the only man alive. You smiled, and all I could think about was seeing if your lips felt as good as they looked. And your hair. Christ, woman. It's wild and natural and makes a man imagine what it would look like after a crazy night of sex."

Her gaze darted over his shoulder toward the pool and the shrill laughter of too many college kids with unlimited booze. "But don't you want someone with a little less wear and tear? I can't compete with girls your age."

Son of a bitch. She thought he was fucking shallow. A

man who couldn't see past vanity and strategically placed highlights. No different from those bastards who thought Photoshopping beautiful women was the answer to a solid bottom line. She may as well have punched him while she was at it. "Right." If he were smart, he'd walk away. Focus on finding a way to fix his business and head home to execute it.

She hugged her stomach, pulled her knees up tight, and curled her toes into the cushion. Something had hurt her. Shaken her confidence as much as his bad business move had shaken him.

"You realize your statement says more about what you think of yourself than it says about me," he said. "I see a woman without pretense. A woman who's real and sexy from the inside out. But if you want to compare yourself to barely legal girls who've never juggled more than how to coordinate the outfits in their closet, or talk about who's dating who, then that's on you."

The wind whipped her hair in front of her face, and she shoved it behind one ear. No clues at all to help him navigate beyond the tight line of her lips and the tension in her body. Either he'd struck a stronger nerve than intended, or she was two seconds away from shooting out of her chair and kicking his ass.

Either way, he'd spoken his truth. He stood. "I'll let you have some time alone. I've got things to take care of this afternoon, but I'd like to have dinner with you. No pressure. No agenda beyond what you're comfortable with. Do you want to join me, or would you rather be alone and discredit everything about you that's amazing?"

Her gaze jumped to his. "That's harsh."

"Also true." He inched closer and cupped her face. Her sun-warmed skin kissed his thumb as he traced her cheekbone. "Whatever you're here for, I'd like to help you find it."

CHAPTER 4

JANIE STROLLED THROUGH the softly lit lobby toward the dining room and let out a slow, calming breath. It was dinner, not a mortal sin. She wished her heart would figure that out and stop its maniacal thumping. Fighting the heat was bad enough. Adding a pulse on overdrive into the mix was too much.

A young couple meandered from the dining room, their fingers twined easily, both of them with carefree smiles. Young and in love. Nothing on the horizon but laughter and building a family.

She remembered those days. Gerald hadn't been able to get enough of her then. When faced with a choice for time with his friends or time with her, he'd always chosen her. When had that changed? Five? Ten years ago? She palmed her stomach, settled her hand on the tiny pooch below her belly button, and sucked in her gut. Damn, she hated when she did that. Like anyone here would notice a middle-aged woman out on her own.

Zade noticed. And he called you sexy.

She relaxed, pushed back her shoulders, and fiddled with the straps of her sundress. The sales lady had sworn the built in bra was sufficient for her full figure, but it sure felt like she was running around topless.

Inside the bustling dining room, wrought iron chandeliers hung from tall ceilings, the tips of the faux candles turned to full brightness. The walls were painted a pale flamingo color that should have been atrocious, but mixed with the turquoise and gold accents, turned the large space into a cozy party. Tables and chairs were lined up tight on one end and three buffets with everything from salad to dessert filled the other.

Zade stood behind two younger men seated at a round table, his hands anchored on their chair backs as he listened to their conversation. His blue button down with rolled up sleeves and khakis were a far cry from the rest of the men at the table, whose rumpled polos and long shorts were probably the only decent attire they'd packed.

He looked up and stopped mid-sentence. His smile shifted from open, easy laughter, to somewhere between pride and sin. He clapped one of the men on the back, never breaking his stare, and left his friends behind.

Catcalls and laughter rang out from table.

Zade kept prowling, his lasered focus so intense she couldn't decide whether to thank God she'd braved the invitation, or run like hell for her room. He crowded close and cupped the back of her neck. "You came."

The way he said it made her wonder if he'd somehow installed a camera in her room. She hadn't surrendered to the need for release, still too hung up on relegating herself to Dirty Old Woman status, but every time she replayed the feel of his hands on her back, she'd come close.

She couldn't remember the last time Gerald had touched her that way. With so much feeling and intimacy it rattled every nerve ending.

His heat filtered through her cotton sundress, and his light, citrusy cologne was one-hundred percent confident, unapologetic male. The kind that made her want to snuggle close and nestle her nose in the crook of his neck, the rest of the room be damned.

"Hungry?"

A fission of pleasure started at her breastbone and radiated outward. God, did everything that came out of his mouth have to spark dirty thoughts? "Definitely."

He smiled, showcasing model-perfect teeth and steered her to the back of the room and the arched double doors that led outside. "I took a chance and pulled in a favor from Arlo. He saved us one of the tables on the balcony. We can either order off the menu or do the buffet. Your choice."

The loud voices and steady clink of flatware on plates dampened the minute she stepped onto the tile veranda. Tables with midnight blue tablecloths were nestled at each end for optimum privacy, with fluttering candles inside hurricane holders in the centers. The sun set behind them and cast the horizon in deep indigo.

She sat in the chair he held out for her and grinned at him as she smoothed her napkin across her lap. "The perks of knowing the owner aren't to be discounted."

He paused beside his chair and rubbed the heel of his hand above his sternum. She'd seen him do that a lot. Usually before he whipped out some profound statement that left her dumbfounded. The wind tousled his longish hair and the candlelight sparked in his soft blue eyes. "Not sure it's to my benefit to point this out, but you're flirting."

A sharp burn stung her cheeks, but she kept her chin up and held his gaze. Stupid blush. Being a redhead was hell. "Could be flirting. Could be maximizing resort connections. Perspective is everything."

That panty-dropping smile of his whipped back into place. She'd have to snap a picture of it before she went home and show it to Mckenna. She'd caption it, *Tread carefully, cross your legs, and don't believe anything when you see this expression.*

Zade lifted his chin and caught the attention of a passing waiter. "I wasn't sure you'd show," he said to Janie.

"I wasn't sure I would either."

He sat back in his chair, head tilted, waiting in that patient way of his. With his uncanny composure, he should have been a counselor or psych professional.

She straightened the knife beside her plate. "I thought about what you said." And about his touch. "You were absolutely right. It was a reflection of my own self-confidence."

"You don't strike me as the kind of woman who normally lacks self-confidence."

No, not normally. Not before Gerald had shaken her well-ordered world and left her staggering through the devastation. Every time she told the story, the burn got worse. And the pity. Damn it, she hated the pity in people's eyes.

Still, he'd told his story. Maybe sharing with a stranger would be therapeutic. "To tell you the truth, I never thought too much about my appearance until recently."

Zade propped his elbow on the arm of his chair and dragged his thumb along his lower lip. His eyes glinted, a silent dare for her to keep going.

"Last week I turned forty and signed my divorce papers." Talk about diving in headfirst. Absolutely zero wind up on the delivery.

Zade's eyebrows shot high, but in more of a *you don't say* way than in shock. He waited for the waiter to set their water and fresh bread in place, then picked the basket up and offered her a roll. "Busy week."

She took one and set it aside. "Yes, well, I'm not including the nine months it took to get to an agreement I'd actually sign. Twenty-two years of marriage takes a while to untangle."

The waiter returned with a chilled bottle of white and an

uncorked red. "*Blanco, o tinto?*"

Zade lifted one eyebrow in silent question.

"Red, please," Janie answered.

The waiter filled her wineglass and looked to Zade for his choice.

"*Tinto para me, también.*"

Another note for Mckenna. *Young men with a mind for foreign languages are a sexual hazard. Seek shelter at the first opportunity.*

He circled his wineglass. God, his hands were big. Long fingers. Powerful. No wonder they'd felt so good. "Did you want the divorce?"

A lash on her heart, as raw and sudden as the day Gerald first uttered the idea. "No. He came home on a Friday night, disappeared into the bedroom for about thirty minutes, and came out with a suitcase. In less than three sentences, he upended what I'd thought was a perfect world."

"Tell me about it."

"About him leaving?"

"No, about your perfect world. What was it like?"

The ocean breeze swept across her nape. The scent of salt and a trace of citronella from the tiki torch fluttered in behind it. "A home. A comfortable routine. Two, mostly well-adjusted, kids. All of our needs met and most of our wants." Dreams and goals from so many years rippled through her mind. "Mckenna starts college next year. We'd have finally had the house to ourselves. Been able to take the trips we said we'd take."

"Where did you want to go?"

"Exploring." She sighed, letting go of the memories. "At least, that's what I wanted. To see how other people live. Other cultures. To see if the places I'd read about in books matched my imagination."

"When did you get married?"

"I was eighteen. Fresh out of high school." She sipped her wine. "It's the one thing I've encouraged my daughter not to do. Not because I regretted my marriage, but because I didn't see the things I wanted to before I committed to raising a family. I want both my kids to experience as much life as they can before they settle down."

The questions kept coming, all of them light and comfortable topics. Janie answered between ordering and eating. How Thomas would probably stay in school three years longer than she or Gerald wanted or planned to support. How Mckenna would probably finish college six months early from sheer impatience to tackle the world. Where Janie would travel to first if she won the lottery, and what she liked best about raising kids.

She tucked her spoon into what was left of her flan and stifled a moan. "What about you? How'd you end up taking sexy pictures of women in their bedrooms?"

"My mom swears it was divine guidance from the universe."

"Your mom?"

He laughed and eased back into his chair, and stretched his long legs out to one side. "I know. Sounds deviant, doesn't it?" He anchored his elbow on the arm of his chair and rubbed his chin. "It was a complete accident. I was in my first year of college, aimed for a business degree. I'd always had a thing for pictures, but wasn't diehard about it. I just seemed to take good ones. Tried to capture the things I found beautiful.

"Anyway, I was home and visiting with my mom and one of her friends at the kitchen table. Her friend was down on herself, frustrated she wasn't seeing results from some new diet she'd devoted a ton of time and energy to. I told her I didn't understand why the hell she was on one anyway. She said, 'Because I'm thirty-three and don't have a man yet. I've got to keep my figure or I'll end up an old maid.'"

He shook his head and grinned. His distant gaze refocused and latched onto Janie. "Really, she had an amazing figure. I don't know where she got such a stupid idea."

Oh, she knew. So did every other woman over the age of

thirty who'd found their first wrinkle or gray hair. "And?"

"We argued. I told her I could prove it. That I'd give her photographic evidence she was as sexy as any twenty-five year old in the same situation. She took the bet."

"You took them in a bedroom?"

"Well, technically I took them in her house and she was wearing a bathing suit. She was so damned excited after the first time, she suggested the boudoir thing. My mom and her friend couldn't keep their mouths shut, and before I knew it, I had a side job to help pay for college."

"You captured the parts of them that were beautiful."

"Everything's beautiful when you focus on the right things."

Janie shuddered, and her lungs seized. He might be a lot younger than her, but he had a profoundly old soul.

He stood, laid his napkin on the table, and offered his hand. "Let's take a walk."

Such a simple request, and yet a tingle bubbled up inside her. Like the walk equated with a swan dive off a tropical cliff into perfect Caribbean waters. She placed her hand in his and followed him down a stairway to one side of the balcony.

The beach stretched out before them, and a large boat with white lights marking its outline floated on the dark ocean. A perky pop song sounded from somewhere behind them, muted by the dining room walls.

"Shoes." He sat on the edge of a raised concrete flowerbed, kicked off his worn, high quality loafers, and rolled up his pant legs. "There's a mandatory barefoot stroll on the beach with every resort date night."

"Is this a date?"

He grinned up at her and a rakish lock of hair fell over his breathtaking eyes. "I showered, put on decent clothes, and fed you. Next on my agenda is getting you comfortable enough, you let me sample your lips the same way you tackled dessert. So, yeah. It's a date."

A tremor wracked her and shimmied straight between her legs. Remembering the feel of his hands on her at the beach had made dressing for dinner a challenge. Processing now what his lips might feel like nearly incapacitated her. She kicked her flirty coral espadrille wedges off and hooked them with two fingers. "I've never been on a date with a younger man before."

He wrapped his arm around her and steered her to the beach, his devious smile doing funny things to her insides. "Everyone deserves a chance to be daring in paradise, don't you think?"

Indeed. And she still didn't know how old he was. "Just how daring am I being?"

He lifted his eyebrow.

"You're old enough to have made it through college," she said. "So I know I won't be carted off for any illegal actions in the morning, but I'm trying to gauge how high my Dirty Old Woman factor will rate."

"I think the new slang is cougar."

Now that he mentioned it, she had heard her son mention the term a time or two, though she'd never thought it would apply to her. "Okay. Cougar. So, how old?"

"Twenty-six." He angled his head and studied her in the moonlight. "And more than capable of pleasuring my date when I get her home."

Translation: Naked, tangled, and sweaty. Her sex clenched so hard, it was a wonder she didn't face plant in the sand mid-stride. And how the heck was she supposed to respond to something like that?

"You never said what brought on the divorce," he said.

Thank God for topic changes. This one might not be all that much easier, but at least with full disclosure, she could address the whole sex-probably-won't-work expectation up front. "He fell in love with someone else." Swallow. Deep breath. Relax through it. "A younger woman."

He stopped. "Is that why you started doubting yourself?"

The stars sparkled bright in the midnight blue sky and the easy ocean breeze caressed her bare skin. Peaceful and perfect. The first safe haven she'd found in months. "I've had one lover in my life. My husband. Everything I knew about my sexuality, my goals, my future, was tied to him. To our kids. Since I was eighteen, I haven't had one thought, one decision, where I didn't factor in the impact my actions would have on my husband or my children. Gerald leaving me for someone so much younger? Yeah, it jarred my self-confidence."

She swiped a long line in the sand with her toe and shrugged. "So, you might want to re-think your endgame of getting me into bed. I'm not nearly as worldly or experienced as you might think."

He widened his stance and stuffed his hands deep in his pockets. "You make it sound like I have a different woman in my bed every night."

Shoot. Not at all the way she'd intended the message to come out. "I meant worldly and experienced in a good way. Though, Arlo did mention your swagger and suave moves."

He cocked his head and scratched his chin. That lopsided, ornery smile of his crept into place. "What Arlo failed to mention was my mother's unconventional influence. He's right. I get along great with women, but that doesn't mean I sleep with them all. Most of what I love about women I learned from watching my mom."

Sexy, responsible, insightful, and held his mother in high esteem. The more she learned about him, the more he lured her in, as gripping as the ocean's riptide.

He eased closer and pulled her to him, his confident, yet soothing touch a welcome anchor. "But I also learned from watching my dad. The way he treated her. Valued her. When he touched her, kissed her, it was powerful. Fucking art in motion."

Oh, yes. Definitely in trouble and teetering on surrender.

He cupped the back of her neck. His fingers seared her

skin, radiating an amazing warmth. "Sex is the single most intimate connection we can make with another person. I don't engage with just anyone. Won't cheapen it with something that's surface deep or with someone I don't feel a connection to."

"So, at the beach when you said you wanted to see me——" God, she couldn't even say it out loud. "You know."

"That I wanted to see the look on your face when you come?" He tightened his grip on her neck and his voice dropped to a delicious rumble. "I said it because the first time I looked at you my world tilted. That's a connection, and I want more."

CHAPTER 5

OH, THAT LOOK. Lips parted just enough to let a man slip his tongue inside. Eyes wide and glossy, pupils so dilated the hazel barely showed. Zade couldn't decide if Janie wanted to bolt, or take him to the sand and go at him right here.

She had a wild streak, for sure. It burned behind her gaze, sharp and sassy, but was tamed behind what sounded like a lifetime of expected behavior. How much would it take to set that passion free? To rile her enough to let loose and give herself free rein?

He stroked the length of her arms, and laced his fingers with hers. "I want to show you something."

She swallowed and lifted her chin. "Show me what?"

Christ, that voice. Scratchy and broken. A dirty-thoughts and I'm-pretty-damned-close-to-losing-it-even-if-I-know-better voice. At this rate, she'd make him come like a sixteen year old with a stolen Playboy before he'd so much as kissed her.

He moved beside her, putting the ocean at their backs. "Uncle Arlo set you up with a pretty nice room, but this one's the best."

He couldn't have framed the setting any better with his camera. Tucked at the deepest point of the cove with palm trees and tropical plants on all sides, save the beach, was his bungalow. Moonlight poured onto the mostly thatched roof, a big skylight in the center. The bungalow had weathered teak wood walls with an oversized sliding glass door across the front, and skinny native tree trunks held the patio's overhang upright.

Janie paced forward a few steps, scanned the private inlet, and then glanced back toward the rest of the resort. "The Stargazer Bungalow."

"You've got a good memory." And an eye for details. Something they had in common. He steered her up the scarred wood slat porch and tossed his loafers on the wide porch swing. "The couple Arlo and Dahlia bought the place from years ago lived here. You can't fully appreciate Gypsy Cove until you see this particular room."

"But he said it's occupied."

"He's right." Zade opened the sliding glass door and waved her in. "By me."

The foot she'd lifted to walk across the threshold went back to the deck. "This is your place?"

"For five more nights, it is." He jammed his hands in his pockets and fought back a chuckle. "I realize what I'm about to say is the height of cliché, but there's something I want to show you inside."

Janie busted out laughing, a full, beautiful laugh that brought a firefly kind of peace to the space around them. "You're right." She covered her mouth, chest rattling as she tried to stifle her outburst. "That's pretty bad. Even for a woman who hasn't been on a date in two decades."

A sheer curtain billowed between them. Zade caught it and held it back. "Then cut a guy some slack and go inside."

She studied him and bit her lower lip.

Damn, he wanted a taste. To nip and lick that same spot. Devour her mouth until it was plump and two shades darker than her rose lipstick. "Arlo's a wiry man, but he and Dahlia would castrate me if I hurt any woman, let alone, a guest. And that's assuming my mother didn't do the job first. But there's no pressure. If you'd rather wait, we can go back up —"

"I'm fine." She took a breath and met his stare head on. "To be clear though, don't expect anything more than a visitor. When I'm ready to leave, I'm leaving."

He nodded, but on the inside he pulled a fist pump and gave himself a high five.

"It's lovely." She paused in the middle of the bungalow, scanned the open floor plan, and meandered toward the small, but well-appointed kitchen along one side. "So what did you want to show me?"

Damn. If she'd laughed before, his next pitch would put her over the edge. He tried to couch his smile, but couldn't hide the lip twitch. He motioned to the raised section along the back of the bungalow and the king size bed in the center. "If you want the full effect, you need to lie on the bed."

She spun to face him, one eyebrow cocked high.

"Seriously," he said. "Swear to God, I'll keep my distance."

Strolling into the living area, she swept her gaze along the cobalt blue sofa and love seat and pursed her lips.

"I'll make you a promise," he said. "The only way I'm getting in bed with you is if you invite me in. Deal?"

She dragged her nails along the chenille armrest, contemplated the beach behind him through the open sliding glass doors a moment, and nodded. "Fine. I'll play." She dropped her shoes and purse on the thick Spanish tiles and padded up the steps to the bed. "Any particular side?"

Guess he'd found a way to rile her after all. And thank God for that because spunky looked damned good on her.

Fire and spirit. Flame and snap. He shook his head. "Wherever is comfortable, so long as I can watch."

She planted her fists on her hips, studied the bed, shrugged, and went for the closest side. Despite her moxie, she settled carefully, mindful of the taut, neatly made covers. She snuggled down, rested her head on the pile of pillows, and laid her hands on her belly, one on top of the other. "Okay. Ready."

The laugh jumped out faster than he could catch it. "Spoken like a true sacrificial virgin." He ambled up the stairs.

The fingers on her top hand tightened.

He strolled to the nightstand beside her and reached for the small box mounted on top. "Look up."

She gauged him for a good long pause, and lay back.

He pressed the red toggle switch on the box.

A muted metal click echoed through the room and a light, motorized whir kicked in behind it. Moonlight slanted above the headboard, a sliver at first, stretching inch by slow inch, bathing Janie in its pearlescent glow.

Janie sucked in a sharp breath and her eyes widened. "It's like a giant moon roof."

"More or less." The motor click-click-clicked, signaling it had reached the end of its track, and Zade punched the toggle back to neutral.

"The Stargazer bungalow." She rolled her head, and looked at him. "I'd never put the cover up."

Zade chuckled and crossed to one of two bedside gold club chairs. "You say that now, but around five thirty in the morning, you'd be singing a whole different tune." He eased into the deep cushions and sat back, arms on the armrests and knees wide.

Janie scrunched deeper into the pillows and drew her knees up at the same time. The moon did gorgeous things to her rich coloring, turning the contrast of her red hair and his white sheets into a sultry work of art. Fuck. He needed his camera and about ten memory cards.

Yeah, like that won't make her hightail it back to her room.

She sighed and curled her toes. "You know, it's not too much different from my house in Allen."

His heart jolted and he snapped from languidness to high alert. "Allen?"

"Mmm hmm." She dipped her chin and met his gaze. "Texas. Just outside of Dallas." She lolled back on the pillows, gaze aimed at the stars and a dreamy expression on her face. "Our place—" Her mouth tensed. "My place is on the outskirts of town. Not a lot of development so you don't get as much of the city lights."

A whopping thirty-five minutes tops from his place in Uptown. Son of a bitch. He could see her more than just this week, assuming they could get past her age hangup and she was interested.

She rolled to her side and propped her head up with one hand. Her hair was wild and free around her, all waves and layers. The kind of image that begged a man to dive in and take over. "It's funny. We've lived there for nearly five years and I've spent more time outside in the last nine months than I spent the whole time before that. I can sit on the back porch for hours. Just a glass of wine, my Adirondack chair, and lots and lots of thoughts."

A smart and thoughtful woman with an eye for details, and who was sexy as hell. The universe couldn't have spun a better scenario.

And she only lived thirty-five minutes away.

She smoothed the comforter. "What are you thinking?"

God, he wanted her to touch him like that. To feel her hair trail against his skin while she worked her lips up and down his body. His voice caught a little on the tension in his throat. "I'm thinking I wish my camera was in my hand instead of in my closet. I'm thinking there's no way in hell I can take it out of the closet without scaring you off. And so, I'm thinking it's best I commit every damned detail of you stretched out on my bed to memory while I've got the chance."

He lifted his hips a fraction and adjusted his cock. It was either that or cut off circulation to the one part of his body demanding the bulk of his blood flow. "Mostly though, I'm thinking I'd give anything for you to invite me to crawl across the bed and make damned sure the only thing you can do is feel."

Janie froze, every muscle locked solid and her breath stifled. The only thing actively working was her heart, which after its initial stumble, had taken off at a gallop.

So tempting. So terribly tempting.

The shadows around him accented the sharp angles of his jaw and nose, and his voice dropped to a grumble. "Talk to me, Janie."

And tell him what? That she wanted what he wanted as bad as he did, but she was terrified to give the green light? That she wasn't sure she could take the disappointment in his eyes if things got serious and he saw what a quality sundress could hide? "What do you want to know?"

"Tell me what you want."

Touch. Passion. Contact. Skin. It all rushed in at once and seized her thoughts.

"One word. One thing at a time." His posture was loose, those powerful hands of his relaxed against the wide gold armrests, but the air around him seemed super-charged. So much so, she could almost scent a summer thunderstorm.

She swallowed and tried to catch her breath. Her answer leapt to her tongue, ready for launch, then stalled. Damn it to hell, she was a living, breathing human, not some freakish deviant. Why couldn't she say what she wanted? Just own it. It was one night. One chance she may never get again. "A kiss."

His fingers dug into the plush upholstery.

The surf crashed against the shore and amplified the tense moment, the sound as bold and passionate as the man watching her.

He stood and padded to her side of the bed.

With every step, her heartbeat surged a notch, and a deep, needy pulse built in her core.

He unhooked his watch. One of those chunky ones her son had begged her for two Christmases ago. Somehow the silver looked right on Zade. Manly. Effortless and stylish without being overblown.

As he set the watch aside, it clunked on the nightstand.

She fisted the cool, crisp sheets and fought the urge to trace the prominent veins that peeked from beneath his rolled sleeves. To pull him closer and nuzzle where the top two buttons of his shirt parted. To surround herself with his powerful scent.

What had she gotten herself into? Never mind age. Trifling with a man like this was tantamount to dancing in the middle of a giant bonfire bathed in gasoline. Her conscience knew it. Kept tapping at the corner of her oxygen-starved thought processes, but every other part of her thrummed and begged to writhe in the flames.

His gaze devoured her, bright blue and bold as a spring sky, framed by loose blond bangs. He straddled her thighs and caged her with his arms, holding himself above her, not touching. "A kiss." He dipped closer, and inhaled deep. "Want to point out, you didn't put any restrictions on your request."

A shudder rippled through her, the sensual sound of his breath and the timbre of his voice resonating like a physical stroke. A simple brush of sensation behind each ear and down her neck.

He traced the line of her lips with his own, close enough to tickle and tease, but not nearly enough to give her what she craved. "You didn't say how…" His warm breath

46

fluttered against her face. "…or where." He licked her lower lip and lifted his gaze to hers. "I'll take that to mean I get to taste all of you."

Contact.

Full, firm, delicious contact. Not a peck before bed. Not a lackluster pretense of interest, but a kiss in the truest sense. Consuming and wild.

His tongue swept past her lips, demanding and merciless. Tasting, licking, nipping her parted mouth until she thought she'd drown in the pleasure. He cruised the line of her jaw with his lips, sampling her skin with tiny flicks of his tongue along the way. "You want more?"

She rolled her head to one side and arched her neck to make way for his devious mouth. He wanted her to think? Now? Thoughts were the last thing she wanted to process. Not with her body languid and pulse pounding.

His teeth scraped the tender shell of her ear, and his voice rumbled deep. "Got a death grip on my hair and the way your hips are moving makes me want to strip you naked and put my mouth to good use somewhere else." He kissed a path down her neck. "Tell me, Janie. You want my weight? My touch?"

Dangerous. So damned dangerous. A line she couldn't cross back from. Her body practically sang beneath him. Demanded more of everything he offered, and didn't give a damn about consequences and awkward morning afters.

He lifted his head, virility pouring off his sharp features. This wasn't a boy. This was a man. A man who wanted her. Desired her enough to wade through all her tangled issues and hang-ups. To take his time and make her feel more alive than she'd felt in forever.

Why shouldn't she ask for what she wanted? She was a grown woman, more than capable of facing tomorrow morning or any other day. She unclenched the back of his head and savored his broad shoulders through his starched shirt, all primal heat and strength beneath her palms. "I didn't come prepared for this."

His gaze dropped to her mouth, then back up to her eyes. "No pressure. Only what makes you feel good." He shifted away.

"Wait." Janie stopped him, digging her nails deep. She trailed her fingers down his throat and rested her palm above his chest. His heartbeat thrummed, solid and steadier than hers, but powerful all the same. "I meant I didn't anticipate precautions. I haven't needed to before. Didn't think we'd—"

"Stop." He captured her hand, lifted it to his lips, and nipped the pad of her middle finger. The contact zinged down her arm and detonated in her belly.

Keeping his eyes on her, he reached to the nightstand and opened the top drawer. He plunked a box of condoms on the edge. "I was a first-rate Boy Scout." Still withholding his weight, he re-centered himself above her. "And before you go wondering, that's a brand new box I picked up after I left you on the beach. Prayed the whole time I wasn't jinxing myself."

"That's a big box."

"Positive thinking." He kissed her. Slow at first, then deeper, nudging her back to mindless euphoria. "Tell me, Janie." He nipped her lower lip and licked to sooth it. "Tell me you want this and I'll spend the rest of the night finding every way I can to make you feel good."

She tugged his shoulders, urging him to her, needing the press of his hard body against hers, the scent of him on her skin.

"Huh uh," he muttered.

God, she was drowning and on fire all at once. Desperate for air, with too many clothes, and not enough touch.

His voice vibrated against her lips. "Say it and I'll give you what you want."

"I want this." It felt like a confession, the weight of worry and fear dissipating as soon as her whisper slipped free. She might regret it later, but she was done with second-guessing herself. Fisting her hands in his hair, she forced more courage into her voice. "I'm scared to death, but I want this. I don't want to think. I don't want to talk. I just want to feel."

A wicked smile split ear to ear and his low, rich voice rattled every nerve ending. "What Janie wants, Janie gets."

He swept in. Lips to lips, hand to the back of her head, and body to body. He growled against her mouth and ground his hips against her. "Feel that?"

Heck, yes, she did. One hundred percent virile male, fully engaged and ready for action. And it felt fantastic. Liberating, even as he pinned her against the mattress.

He undulated lower and his cock raked the top of her mound, the pressure and her sundress dragging sensuously against her silk panties. "Stroked one off yesterday and twice today, and I'm still hard enough to drive nails."

He thumbed her nipple through the light fabric, the tight point so sensitive, the touch shot clear to her toes. "Tell me the truth." He cupped her breast and the heat of his palm seared straight through her dress. "Have you touched yourself since yesterday?"

"No." A serious miscalculation she wished like hell he'd hurry up and rectify. She pressed her thighs together and rubbed her mound against him. God, she was wet, her panties clinging to her labia in a way that only made the ache between her legs worse.

He peeled the dress straps off her shoulders and teased the exposed swells of her breasts. "You think about it?"

The snippets she'd allowed alone in her room blasted front and center in her mind. Zade naked above her, buried deep, her hands splayed across and sampling his chest. She squeezed her eyes shut and tried to kick the image.

He chuckled and peeled her dress an inch or two further, licking the space he'd exposed. "I'll take that as a yes."

The fabric barely covered her nipples, the rasp so erotic she almost begged him to free her completely. To sooth her need with his hot mouth. She arched an offering. So close. Almost there.

"Tell me what you thought about." He sat back on his heels and ghosted his knuckles down her sternum.

Damn it, he wasn't making this easy. Good, but not easy. She touched the hollow of his throat and dragged until her fingers met the first button on his shirt. "Your body." She flipped the button free and slipped her hand inside. Warm, tight skin stretched over strong, lean muscles. "How it would look. How it would feel."

His eyes darkened and he gripped the sides of her dress. "Think we had the same fantasy." He pulled the fabric down to her waist, his gaze trailing with it.

The breeze through the open door teased her tight breasts, and her nipples beaded to the point they ached.

"Beautiful." He tugged her dress lower. Past her hips, her ankles, then tossed it to the floor. With his palms at her hips, he pressed a reverent kiss above her navel, eyes feasting on every inch of her. Slowly, he met her stare and traced the lace waistband of her panties. "Perfect curves and creamy skin." He dragged his thumb down the center of her mound and stroked her clit through the silk. "I'll bet you taste even better."

Oh, dear Lord, imagining those lips on her sex. She moaned and flexed into the perfect pressure his fingers created. Slick friction. Too much and not enough.

"Fuck, yes, I love that sound." He whipped her panties down her legs and crawled between her thighs. Planting one hand beside her head, he held himself above her, eyes locked to hers, and slipped his fingers through her slit. "So wet." He slicked the moisture up and around her clit, then teased her entrance. "First time, just like this. Where I can watch you come."

"First time?" As in more than one? Was he crazy?

"First time." He grinned, more feral and determined than playful. "As in several." He thrust a finger deep.

She whimpered and lifted to meet his strokes, grinding against the heel of his hand. Maybe not so crazy after all.

The man had a way with his fingers, slicking inside her with confident, demanding strokes.

"Want more of those sexy noises." He added a second finger, pumping slow and steady. "Want to feel your pussy squeeze me and hear you shout while you do it."

Her muscles quivered, a powerful release so close and bright it threatened to burn.

"Look at me, Janie." His cock pressed against her hip, the rough abrasion of his khakis sinful on her bare skin. "Look at me and let me watch it take you."

She pried her eyes open.

His blazing blue gaze shone down on her. Hungry. Powerful. "That's it." He angled his wrist, nudging the sweet spot inside, and thumbed her clit. "Right. Fucking. There."

"Yes." Ragged and broken, she cried out as her sex clutched him. Over and over, one delicious pulse after another. Perfect. Wicked and all consuming. She rode each thrust, her hips lifting and falling to drag the sensation out as long as it could go.

She clasped his shoulders, lust and the after effects of her shouts straining her voice. "Zade."

"Right here." He kissed her temple, then skated his lips along her cheekbone. His movements eased in intensity, but kept a slow, easy pace. "Unbutton my shirt, babe. Don't want to let you go yet."

Oh, God. He was still dressed. "You didn't—"

"Got exactly what I wanted." He deepened his strokes. "Gonna get more as soon as you get this shirt off of me."

Shirt off. Right.

The pressure of his thumb on her clit increased and he licked and sucked the line of her neck.

"Ohhh." She tugged and fumbled with the buttons. "Can't focus when you do that."

"Rip the damned things." His tongue circled her nipple, breath hot against the hard peak. "Don't care how, just get it off."

The last button slipped free and she shoved it past his shoulders.

He growled and sat back, gaze locked on his busy fingers buried deep. "Touch yourself."

Her hips flinched and broke rhythm for all of a millisecond. "What?"

His eyes snapped to hers. "Just got you going. Not about to let you ease down yet." His mouth tilted in a naughty grin. "Come on, Janie. You yelled like a wild woman. We both know what you've got bottled up in there. Let go and own it."

Let go. Own it. Why the hell not?

She unfisted the sheet and caressed her belly.

"Oh, yeah." He shrugged one arm from his shirt, the rest dangling from his still occupied hand between her legs. With every move of his wrist, his muscles flexed, tanned flesh rippling in the moonlight.

He kept at it, seemingly mesmerized by her hesitant fingers, until they dipped close to his.

He pulled free.

Janie groaned at the loss and surged to replace it.

He popped his fingers in his mouth and sucked her release like it was the sweetest treat he'd ever received. "Hell, yeah. Want more of that, too."

Tossing off the last sleeve, he maneuvered off the bed and unfastened his belt in quick, sharp movements. He shoved his pants past his hips and reached for the box on the nightstand.

Sweet mother of all that's holy.

The crinkle of foil dimly registered, but Janie couldn't tear her eyes off his cock. Thick, heavily veined, and jutting tall. Her knees widened of their own accord, breath huffing to match a marathoner's.

"Just like that." Zade fisted his shaft and stroked. Once. Twice. "Fuck, that's sexy as hell." He rolled the condom into place and crawled between her thighs, gaze locked on her steady strokes. Sliding his hands beneath her hips, he lifted her up. "My turn."

"Yes!" She clutched the back of his head, hands fisted in his hair. "Zade."

His growl vibrated against her flesh and his tongue lashed through her folds. Scorching. Branding her with his wicked mouth on her clit.

Another climax billowed up, slower than the first, but bigger. Powerful enough to leave her boneless. She tugged his hair, a tiny part of her embarrassed at the savage treatment, but the rest of her desperate to be filled. "Zade, now. Please."

His head whipped up, lips shiny with her release. "Now what?" He crept up her body, his heavy shaft bobbing with each movement. "Tell me."

To hell with reservations. With right and wrong. Age and worry. "Fuck me." It rolled off her tongue, smooth and easy. Empowering and bold. "Fill me up and fuck me hard. Now."

His feral smile stretched ear to ear. "Wild." He worked the flared crown through her folds and lined himself up. "Knew you would be."

He surged forward, filling and stretching her in one thrust. So full. Tight. Perfect.

She wrapped her legs around his hips and dug her heels into his flanks. Beneath her palms, his biceps and shoulders contracted and released, bunched bands of steel with barely leashed power.

Movement flashed in her periphery. The dresser mirror, Zade pistoning into her willing flesh. The muscles in his ass flexed with each surge, the sight pushing her to the top of her release.

"Look at me." Zade laced his fingers with hers and pinned them on either side of her head. His voice was thick and grated, his breath as heavy and heated as hers. "Like you watching me take you, but this time I want your eyes. Want you to come knowing who's inside you. Who's taking you there."

He shifted his hips and drilled deep, rasping her clit with each thrust. "Come on, Janie. Let go. Come for me and take me with you."

His eyes. So intense and locked on her.

"Zade." Her pussy clenched, release seizing her thoughts and senses in its merciless grip.

He growled above her, hips hammering against her flesh, and head thrown back, revealing corded muscles and strained veins.

She shook, clutching him for dear life as she rode the sensations. Her wild pulse, each contraction of her core, each flex of his cock. Bliss. Primitive, incredible bliss. Carnal and yet so perfect, it rattled an untouched part of her. A sleeping side of herself she hadn't even known existed.

Slowly, he gave her his weight. Their skin was slick with sweat. He explored the curve of her shoulder with leisurely, soft kisses and rocked his hips against her in easy strokes.

She trailed her fingertips up and down his spine, her mind languid and peaceful in a way she hadn't felt in years, if ever. A shiver wriggled through her and a hairline crack zigzagged through her defenses. He'd been right. This was special. Maybe not meant for more than their time together, or even one night. But it was a connection. And it was profound.

CHAPTER 6

SNUGGLING INTO THE crisp cool sheets, Janie rolled to her side and hugged her pillow. The scent of citrus and wood surrounded her. And man. Lots and lots of sinful man.

Wait a minute.

She clenched the sheet to her chest and sat upright. Butter yellow walls, the quiet cove just outside, and a skylight overhead.

Zade's room.

She buried her face in the pillow and groaned. Dear Lord, she'd slept with a man fourteen years younger than her. Not dreamt it, but actually done it. And it had been outstanding. Not at all the awkward disaster she'd been afraid of. If anything, Zade had seemed as blown away as she'd been.

She popped her head up. No running water or shuffling sounded from the bathroom and the kitchen was empty. She scrambled off the bed, tugging the top sheet with her, and wrapped it around her. The ocean breeze filtered through the open glass door and the porch swing creaked with each sway. No one on the private beach, either.

She plodded to the tiny kitchen. All clean, no coffee going. A few travel magazines sat on the coffee table and a phone charger lay coiled and ready for action on the end table. On the bedroom dresser was a small container full of Mexican coins and what she thought were memory cards.

She plunked down on the edge of the bed. 10:14 glowed a soft blue from a baseline black alarm clock. No note. Not anywhere. Goose bumps prickled down her arms and her throat tightened. Maybe it hadn't been as outstanding for him. What if he'd left to avoid a clumsy morning scene?

Shit.

She snatched her clothes off the floor. Not a big deal. She was a big girl and more than capable of handling this situation in a calm, classy manner.

Oh, who the heck was she kidding? She'd slept with him after barely two days, and was almost old enough to be his mother. Classy had left the building a long time ago.

Ugh. She'd heard the expression "walk of shame," but it sounded a lot funnier when she wasn't the one doing it. She tossed her dress on the couch near her shoes and untangled herself from the sheet.

Across the room, a brown leather stationery folder lay near the corner of the writing desk. A note would be classy. God knew, a little something from him would've dialed her angst down a bit. Even something trite like, *It was fun*, would have been helpful.

She re-tucked the sheet around her and shuffled over to the desk, the starched linens hissing on the cool tile floors behind her. Like everything else at the resort, the stationery had a quirky, yet quality feel to it. Deckled edges in a bold Robin's egg blue. She white-knuckled the pen and nibbled the end of it.

Thank you so much for the lovely dinner. I had a wonderful time.

* * *

Good Lord. She wasn't writing thank you cards. She wadded the sheet up and tossed it over by her dress. She needed something meaningful, but that let him know she got the message loud and clear. One night. No more.

Last night meant everything. I'll treasure it forever.

Gah. Meaningful, not lovesick and melodramatic.

She crumbled that one up, threw it over with the first, and pulled out a fresh sheet. She tapped the pen on her lips. God, no wonder he hadn't left a note. This morning after crap wasn't as easy as it looked.

Footsteps sounded on the patio, followed by a soft clatter.

Janie twisted in her chair as Zade strode through the door.

"You're up." His smile shone as cheerfully as the midmorning sun and his beach attire was back in place, shirtless with leather flip-flops and board shorts. Though this time he'd gone with a turquoise pair that drew twice as much attention to his eyes.

His gaze shuttled from the stationery in front of her, to her clothes and the wads of paper beside it. The smile dimmed. "You're leaving?"

"Well, I…" *Wasn't sure what the protocol was? Thought maybe you wanted me to get out?* "I didn't know if you were gone for the day or—" She waved around the room. "Well, I didn't know."

He palmed the spot above his heart, eyes thoughtful. "You thought I'd bailed." Despite the nature of his comment, he sounded like he thought she was funny.

"This is new to me. I wasn't sure what to think."

He ambled to her dress and plucked the papers from the couch.

Janie shot forward. "Oh, don't read those."

He plopped to the couch, holding the papers away from her. "No, I think this will be fun." He patted his lap. "Come on. I wanna see what you had to say."

"They're horrid. One's a thank you note and I don't know what the other is. Bad Jane Austen, I guess. I gave up before I got too far."

He grabbed her wrist and pulled her across him, encircling her in his arms as he unwrinkled the first page. He chuckled as he read the first. "I take it this is the thank you note?"

She fidgeted and tried to at least make sure she didn't crush his thighs with her weight. "I'm quite good at those."

"I see that." He tossed it to the side and opened the other.

The soft swoosh of ocean waves filled the quiet. Too much quiet.

Janie pushed against Zade's shoulder to stand.

Zade tightened his arms around her and shuttled his thumb beside her hasty scribbles. "Did you mean it?"

Last night meant everything.

She swallowed, the back of her throat and tongue dry enough to make the process a challenge. Either she played it cool, or told him the truth. Considering she'd likely never see him again, pride over truth seemed cowardly. And the night really had been a tremendous gift. "A bit melodramatic in delivery, but yes."

He set the paper aside more carefully than the first, then stretched out beside her on the couch. Zade lay partly over her, his legs tangled with hers. He traced her jawline, gaze moving over her face in a slow, leisurely glide. "I went to get you breakfast."

And she'd naturally thought the worst. "I shouldn't have assumed you'd left so quickly."

His thumb ghosted across her lip. "Says more about you than it does about me, babe." His grin whipped back into place. "Though I'll learn my lesson and be sure I leave a note next time."

Next time. Stupid to pounce on such a small comment so quickly, but her heart practically skipped at the idea. "You got me breakfast?"

His eyelids grew weighted and his gaze locked on her lips.

"Figured you'd be hungry after last night. Besides——" He rolled back and pulled a brochure from his pocket. "I need to keep you fed if we're gonna make it through today."

"What's that?"

He flipped the emerald green paper over and showed the main caption.

Mayan Catamaran Paradise Tours

"You said you wanted to explore." He waggled his eyebrows. "Welcome to day two of your personalized tour experience."

The wide sailboat with its blue and white sails lifted on a wave and dropped in a graceful swoop. Ocean water misted Janie's back and cooled her hot skin. Thank God, Zade had remembered the high-octane sunscreen. Mexico's late afternoon sun wasn't something to trifle with beachside. Splayed out on the trampoline surface between the boat's two hulls, her redhead fair skin was a lightning rod for extra crispy trouble. Especially considering how the skin on display hadn't seen the sun in ages.

How Zade had talked her into wearing a bikini, she still couldn't figure out. She'd bought and packed two at Mckenna's insistence, but never actually thought she'd wear one. Now here she was, on her stomach, back straps untied, and at Zade's mercy for re-tying them.

The trampoline shifted and a shadow slanted over her.

"You still with me?" Zade stretched out on his side next to her, head propped on one hand. The wind had turned his unruly hair into something straight from a surfer god's playbook, and his tan made his white teeth and blue eyes all the more impressive.

"I'm with you." She motioned toward her back. "Tie me back up so I can flip over."

"Flip over without it."

"I will not." She craned her neck over one shoulder toward the man steering their boat. Private tour or not, she wasn't going for no tan lines with an audience. "He's right over there."

"He can't see a thing. I know because I checked." He leaned in. "He also mentioned we've got at least twenty minutes before we're anywhere close to shore and that he'd keep his distance."

"What?"

He busted out laughing, shifted and grabbed a plastic container full of bite-sized fruit. "Come on, babe. We're not the first couple who's taken a private cruise. You're hot, I'm young, and he's smart." He held a piece of pineapple near her lips.

Janie opened her mouth the same way she had countless other times during their six-hour excursion. About the only time she'd fed herself had been at the Isla Mujeres all-you-can-eat buffet, and even then he'd spoon-fed her three different dessert samples. The guy had a serious mouth fixation.

He slipped the fruit inside and dragged his thumb along her lower lip before he drew away. His voice dropped. "Live a little, Janie. No one will know. No one but us."

She couldn't. Just thinking about it made her face flame hot, but the sun and air on her back did feel good. She imagined the sensation on her breasts, out in the open, and a flutter rippled deep in her abdomen.

He smoothed to one side the wisps of hair that had escaped her clip and kissed the back of her neck. "No pressure from me. Only support." His lips slid to her shoulder and nipped her warm skin. "Either way, it's time for you to roll over. I have plans for you later that won't go well with a sunburn, so make the call. You want me to tie you back up or keep the twins free?"

No pressure. No one around but the two of them and a man named Pedro she'd never see again. "You sure he can't see me?"

His fingers tightened on her shoulders and his lips hovered at her ear. "Checked for a reason, babe. Proud as hell to be seen with you, but not at all interested in sharing with Pedro."

One chance. No way would she be able to do this again, and she was always telling her kids not to let opportunities pass.

Zade beamed at her, his gaze full of pride and sparkling to match the sun on the water.

"I can't believe I'm going to do this." God, her voice was deep. Raspy like one of those screen goddess femme fatales.

Zade's grin kicked up a notch. "I can't believe I'm the lucky bastard who's with you." He moved back enough to let her up and reached for her beach bag. "Roll on over, wild woman. Let's give the twins a little one on one time with Father Sun."

She pulled in a steadying breath and rolled to her back.

The sun and wind teased her skin like a mix of warm and cool silk all at once. Her stomach clenched and her nipples hardened. Now she got it. Topless, at least, on a beach had a lot of merit. It felt great. Amazing, bohemian, come-to-momma, kind of great.

A shadow fell across her a second before the trampoline jolted and Zade straddled her, his knees at her hips. He flipped the top on her fifty-plus sunscreen and scowled down at her.

"Something wrong?"

"Tactical error." He studied her another moment then shook his head and squeezed out a handful of lotion. "Nope. I'll do it."

"Oh, Zade. You can't." The tour guide hadn't popped into view, but God only knew what might make him change his mind.

"Can't have the twins out of action," he said, all business. "Either you put on the sunscreen or I do. If it's me, I can hone my thoughts on warming you up for later. If it's you, I'll come in my trunks before you get it rubbed in."

"But, Pedro—"

"Is busy." He smoothed the cool lotion up her rib cage and cupped her breasts. His voice dropped a sexy octave. "As. Am. I."

Holy moly, his hands felt good. She arched into his confident, powerful strokes and bit back a moan. Barely two full days left to her own devices as a single woman, and she was topless on the ocean getting rubbed down by a man fourteen years her junior. Not too shabby. Wrong on so damned many levels, yes, but mmmm. The man knew how to use his hands.

He massaged in the last of the lotion and finished off with a teasing pinch to her nipples. His lungs rose and fell in a deep, ragged pattern. "Gonna have to schedule another private tour tomorrow. Can't finish what I want to do to you in fifteen minutes."

And wasn't that a pity. Another minute and she'd have forgotten about Pedro, the ocean, and anything else in a five-mile area.

He swung himself off her hips and reclined against the raised hull. "Come on over here and lean back on me. If I keep a head-on view of you in the sun like that much longer I'll get us into more than Pedro bargained for."

The idea shouldn't thrill her as much as it did, but the way he looked at her, hungry and ready to toss caution to the wind, fired a heady confidence she'd never felt before.

She crawled toward him, her bare breasts tight and sensitive to each sway of the boat. Settling between his legs, she laid her back against his chest. A long, easy sigh rolled past her lips, tension from the last nine months and God only knew how many years before vaporizing with it.

He gripped her hips and nuzzled her ear. "You're fucking gorgeous. How you don't know that is beyond me."

He sure as heck made her feel that way. Riviera royalty

gorgeous. She stretched a little more, angling to the glorious sun.

He tightened his hold. "Talk to me."

"You get me almost naked on the ocean, work me up, and then ask me to talk?"

"The only way I'll make it to shore is if you keep my dirty mind occupied."

She smiled big enough, her cheeks protested. "Well. Wouldn't want your dirty mind to start something it can't finish. So, what can we talk about?" She wiggled her butt and teased his hard cock pressed against her back.

He hissed and thrust his hips against her.

God, she should be ashamed. "So, you sold your business. What's your next step from here?"

He huffed out a harsh laugh, and his warm breath brushed the back of her neck. "Well, that's one topic to derail my hard-on."

"What?" She tried to turn, but Zade held her in place.

"It's fine. I'm joking. Mostly."

"I didn't mean to bring up something that bothered you."

"Not a bother so much as a frustration." He relaxed beneath her and massaged her shoulders in languid strokes. "I'm mad as hell at myself for signing the deal as it is, but they put a non-compete clause in the contract. I can't engage in any competing business for two years."

He paused for a minute. "I was so caught up in someone wanting to buy the business I'd built…so overwhelmed with what I saw as success, that I didn't realize I was cutting myself short in the long run. Not to mention, they'd crater what I'd created."

"A non-compete that's defendable?" She covered his hands with hers. "No, way. My husband, I mean my *ex*-husband's, been doing contract law in Texas for years. That's got to be one of the hardest clauses to defend. Particularly when you're dealing with a person's livelihood. They can't tell you that you can't work anymore. Even if the clause was defendable, you could do a new spin on your company. Teach other people how to do what you do. Or find a different, unique environment for your photo shoots. There's always a way to work it. Just talk to your lawyer. The laws can't be that much different in California."

"California?"

She peeked up at him. "That's where you live, right? You said the company that bought you out is from California, so I assumed—"

The boat rose and crashed on a steep wave and jiggled her breasts. She shrieked, cupped them, and giggled like a sixteen-year-old. "Okay, the sun feels good, but that's a downside."

Zade covered her hands and growled near her ear. "Trust me when I tell you, that was not a downside. Hell, I hope it's choppy sailing from here to shore."

She whacked his thigh and settled back against him.

"You really think it's that simple?" he said. "Just talking to a lawyer?"

"Oh, I don't know about simple. Lawyers are never simple, but I'd say there's usually a loophole somewhere. Seems like I heard Gerald talk about one company who didn't uphold the quality or the mission of the business, and the seller was able to get the company back for breach of something or other. I don't know what it's called. Seriously, have a lawyer check the contract out. You just need a knowledgeable set of eyes."

Zade unfastened her hair clip and finger-combed the untamed mess.

Easing into his casual touch, Janie closed her eyes and soaked in the moment. The sun, the wind, the steady swish of water spraying as the hull cut a clear path toward home. Oh, if Emmy could only see her now.

"So, you're a free woman now," Zade said. "One kid already in college and another leaving soon. What's your next step?"

Wasn't that the sixty-four thousand dollar question. Or in this day and age, the sixty-four million dollar question. Geez, she was old. "I guess that's what Emmy sent me here for. To figure out what to do next."

"Emmy?"

"My baby sister. She lives as large and loud as the colors she wears, and has never met a stranger. She might be five years younger than me, but I'll swear she's got the spirit of a wise man."

"An old soul."

Janie cackled loud enough, it should have brought Pedro scrambling over the center cabin. "God, don't let her hear you say she's old anything. I've never met a woman more determined to fight the aging process."

"If she's anything like you, she won't have to fight hard." He combed her hair to one side of her neck. "Do you have any places you want to start? Ideas you want to pursue?"

All the peaceful sounds around her reverberated loud as cymbals in her head, and the unfamiliar panic she'd been fighting since Gerald dropped his I've-fallen-in-love-with-someone-else speech surged to full pitch. "I have absolutely no idea."

Zade laced his fingers with hers, comforting without being overbearing.

"The alimony will cover me for as long as I need it to and the house is paid off. Needless to say, Gerald felt obliged to give it to me in the divorce. Still." She shook her head. "Living off him doesn't sit well with me. I want to be a model for Mckenna. To show her it's important for a woman to be able to take care of herself."

"Did you do anything when the kids were growing up? Volunteer anywhere?"

"Oh, yeah," she said. "PTA, church, a few of the sports organizations the kids were involved with. I was quite the take-charge, figure out how to get it done woman."

"So maybe you start there." He edged out from behind

her and met her gaze. "You said you wanted to go back to school. Why not look at a business management degree? Hell, you zoned in on a solution to my problem quick enough."

School. Tests and studying. Class schedules and credit hours. All those things she'd helped her kids with. "You don't think it's too much to take on? I mean, I'd stick out like a sore thumb on any kind of campus."

Zade scoffed. "Hardly. You really think you're the only adult over the age of thirty readjusting their life? I bet half my bachelor's graduating class had at least twelve years on me."

Twenty-six years old, barely out of college, and she'd slept with him. Was running around topless as footloose and fancy free as her sister always encouraged her to be.

"Something wrong?" he said.

"I keep forgetting you're younger than me. You don't act like it." She glanced down at her bare torso. "Well, except when you're trying to talk me out of my clothes."

"Out of curiosity, how old is your husband's new interest?"

"Twenty-four."

"So what's the difference?"

Well, damn. He had her there. "Okay, I'll grant you it's a double standard. But I guarantee you some of the people at church would deem me a cradle robber."

The horizon shifted and her hair slanted across her face as Zade flipped her to her back on the trampoline. "Cradle robber, huh?"

Pedro's voice floated from behind the raised partition shielding them from view. "Five minutes to shore, *señor.*"

Zade studied her a moment, a wicked glint in his eye, then tugged his T-shirt free of the beach bag. He tossed it to her and stuffed her bikini top where the shirt had been. "Then maybe we need to go back to the resort and do some things that would shock them for reasons that have nothing to do with age."

CHAPTER 7

FIVE DAYS INTO her vacation and probably ten pounds heavier, Janie plucked the last bite of the best lobster she'd ever eaten off the tiny tabletop grill and dunked it in a bowl of drawn butter. "You weren't kidding with the food. Thank God I brought mostly sundresses. I won't fit into my shorts by the time I head home."

"You can't come to Fifth Avenue and not eat at La Parrilla. I think it flies in the face of tourist law." Zade rested an arm on the wrought iron balcony rail overlooking the busy street below. No cars were allowed, but tourists strolled thick up and down the many storefronts with everything from cheesy T-shirts to Cuban cigars. "This place looked a whole lot different when I first came to visit Arlo and Dahlia. I'm glad the area's drawing more people, but I hope they can hang on to Gypsy Cove so some of the old feel sticks around."

A ceiling fan with fat blades and a motor big enough to power a small plane whirred above them, making the early evening heat far more bearable. Color surrounded her on all sides. Gold stucco walls trimmed in cobalt blue, terra cotta tile floors with bold yellow suns painted in the center of each square, and red, green, and white Mexican banners crisscrossed on the ceiling.

Lovely. A picture she couldn't imagine ever forgetting. And Zade had given it to her. She nudged her plate away and leaned back in her chair. "I'm stuffed."

"Don't forget the sopaipillas."

She rubbed her stomach like that might somehow make more room. "Oh, no. I need about four hours on the treadmill to offset the chips and guacamole alone. And you knew better than to get me the big margarita. I haven't finished any of the jumbo sized ones yet."

"We'll tackle calorie burn later." He tore the corner off one of the four cinnamon pastries he'd ordered despite that she'd told him not to, and dragged it through a pile of honey. "Right now we've got dessert to enjoy and tacky souvenirs to buy."

The guy had endless energy. For three days in a row, he'd taken her one simple desire to explore new places to heart and surprised her every morning with a new tour. Swimming with dolphins, manatees, and sea lions, a tour of Mayan ruins, and a frigid float down an underground river.

He wiped his fingers and planted his elbows on the table, studying her with a crooked grin. The same amused, yet content expression he'd watched her with since that first day on the beach.

"What?" She straightened and tidied the table. Anything to distract herself from trying to read too much into what his look meant.

"Trying to figure out if I want to give you something or not."

She barked out a laugh loud enough to make the bartender's head whip in their direction. Covering her mouth and waving an apology toward the bar, she said in a lower voice, "You've carted me all over Riviera Maya for the last three days and curled my toes until I slept like the dead for three nights. What else could you want to give me?"

His gaze skimmed down to her breasts, then back up to her eyes. "Curled your toes, huh?"

Okay, maybe the industrial grade ceiling fan wasn't enough for August in Mexico. She fanned herself and shifted in her chair. "Like you don't already know that. If I pump your confidence any higher, half the women at the resort will instantaneously combust."

He ducked his head.

Good grief, was he blushing?

Yep. He looked back up, and a hint of pink dotted his sharp cheekbones. He pursed his lips a minute, thoughtful, and then pulled a folded piece of paper from his pocket. "You know that idea you had? About my business and talking to a lawyer?" He unfolded the papers, and held them so she couldn't see the print. "Well, I called a guy Arlo recommended the next morning while you were still asleep and sent him a copy of the contract. While I was up there I did a little surfing on Arlo's computer for you, too."

"For me?"

The papers bobbed from the steady swirl of the wind above. "So, don't take this as a push, all right? I just thought I'd show you there are a lot of options out there."

He cleared a space between them and smoothed the sheets out so they faced her.

Business Administration. Business Management. Business Technology.

She thumbed through the pages. "These are degree programs."

"Did you know there are fifty colleges offering programs within fifteen miles of Dallas?"

"No." She probably should, with one kid already burning through tuition and another about to start, but Mckenna and Thomas had picked their ideal locations long before she'd ever thought to research.

"Yeah, blew my mind, too. But there are a ton of options out there. And if the classroom thing bugs you out, you can always do an online program. At least to start."

College. At her age. That hadn't been just lip service he'd given her when he'd first mentioned it. "You really think I can do this."

"Uh, yeah." He sat back in his chair, knees wide and hands loose in his lap. "You're a smart woman, Janie. Practically every place we've gone you've jumped in to help people when they needed it. You fix things that need fixing before people even realize something's wrong."

"Pfft. Name one."

"The new hostess when she got the parties waiting for a table confused."

"Well, her trainer shouldn't have left her alone with so many people waiting." She smoothed her napkin out on her lap. "That was just common decency."

He rested his chin on his hand. "What about the couple with the mixed up itinerary at the resort?"

"What about them?"

"You could've waited until Arlo made it up from his office, but you jumped on the business center computer and helped them track down what was wrong."

Hmmm. She had jumped in pretty easily.

"I see you're getting it." He leaned in, pulled one of her hands from the stack of papers, and clasped it. "What I don't think you realize is you do it all the time. Quickly. Without thinking. And always with a smile."

But those were small things. Surely nothing that would translate into a career.

Business Administration: Majors in business administration should expect to focus on learning and developing the skills necessary to plan, organize and manage the many aspects involved in running a business, including business processes and financial analysis. Students will be prepared to excel in a variety of business opportunities in different industries. Potential job titles a graduate of this program might expect to fill: Human resources manager, business analyst, or operations analyst.

Wow. Janie McAlister. In an office. A professional. "But the things I do can't be equated to real world office-type things."

He shuttled his thumb back and forth against the pulse at her wrist. "My attorney called while I was getting ready for dinner. That clause you mentioned, the one that requires the seller to maintain the integrity of the company? Mine has something like that. The attorney thinks I have grounds to get my business back. I don't call that small. And you gave me the direction I needed."

"Oh." Her stomach flipped on his behalf and her heart jolted. She'd really helped him. "I guess that one's a little bigger."

He smiled big enough to flash his perfect white teeth, eyes sparkling. "That one made my fucking day."

The waiter bustled to the table with two young helpers and cleared the dishes. "All finished, *señor*?"

Zade handled the check, taking time to chat with the man, as he did with everyone. No one was a stranger. Everyone was equal. He'd alluded to visually appreciating women and certain aspects of the world when he'd described his business, but he'd sold himself short. Watching Zade watch the world was a beautiful thing in itself. The sharpness in his eyes. The way his gaze scanned the entire picture, capturing every detail. The way his mouth softened and parted when something powerful struck his interest.

"You okay?"

People strolled on either side of them, and a cluster of kids giggled near a storefront where a man made a flamenco string puppet dance to a song on the radio. Talk about inattentive. She'd made it down a flight of stairs and past a thick crowd of diners without realizing where she was. "Sorry. Was off in my head, thinking about your idea."

"Don't follow it if it doesn't feel right. It's what you want that's important. Sounds like you've helped everyone else in your life. Now's a chance for you to figure out what you want."

What she wanted. Three little words that seemed to broaden the universe in one dramatic swoop. Liberating. Powerful. Scary as hell. "Thank you."

His eyebrows dipped in the center. "For what?"

God, she'd misjudged him with the age thing. She'd never met a man so honest. Genuine and giving. Emotionally open and mature. "For helping me with ideas. Seeing me in a different light." More words snagged on the back of her throat. Raw words that would expose more than she should.

Ah, to heck with it. After what he'd given her, a little honesty would be good. "For helping me see I'm still beautiful. That I'm not washed up. That wrinkles and gravity aren't the end of me, just a different part of my story."

He stopped in the middle of the street, pulling her to a stop beside him. Cupping her face on either side, he brushed his thumbs along her cheekbones. "You're not the kind of woman who'll ever be washed up. There's too much light in you. Any man who doesn't want to drown himself in that brightness doesn't deserve the good that comes with it."

Flutters danced in her stomach and her breaths turned shallow. So perfect. A man she could trust and rebuild her world with. To look at the world with a fresh set of eyes.

Except he lived over fifteen hundred miles away.

From behind them, a booming, masculine voice rang out. "Hey, Zade."

Janie spun with Zade.

The man who'd been with Zade the day they met ambled from one of the beach-party dive bars. At his side was a beautiful girl with perfect blond highlights, too much makeup for her naturally pretty face, and not nearly enough clothes. God, help her if Mckenna came home from her first year of college the same way.

Zade offered his hand as the couple strolled up. "Hey,

Devin." He wrapped an arm around her. "You remember Janie."

"Hard not to remember the ball buster." He tipped his head toward Janie, an awkward attempt to be polite and still appear cool in front of his girlfriend, as if he'd hadn't already blown it with the ball buster comment. "How ya doin'?"

"I'm great, thank you." Janie held out her hand to the girl. "I'm Janie McAlister."

The girl gnashed her gum, zigzagged her gaze between Janie and Zade, and shook the hand offered. "Hey. I'm Nelly."

With a beer fisted in his free hand, Devin motioned toward the beach. "We're headin' back to the resort for a poolside party. You guys wanna come?"

Zade glanced at Janie and rubbed his chin. "Um."

Like she'd be any help on this one. Her experience with pool parties usually involved wine and business deals. This one was probably more along the line of beer, loud music, and lots and lots of splashing, with or without the bathing suit. She rolled her lips inward to stifle a grin, and shrugged.

"Yeah, sure," Zade said. "We'll stop by when we get back."

"Cool." Devin chin-lifted at Janie and tugged Nelly closer as they strolled away. "See y'all back at the cove."

They'd barely made it out of earshot before Zade's laughter rumbled around Janie. "You know we don't actually have to go. I doubt they'll even remember it if we do."

"I don't mind. I'll chalk it up to getting an inside track on what my kids are up to at college."

His thumb idly stroked the top of her hand as they strolled toward the taxi line at the end of the street. "You know, not all people his age are like that."

Well, heck. She'd kind of earned that comment, along with the zap to her conscience. She cleared her throat. "It's been brought to my attention by an increasingly reliable source, I might have been guilty of lumping all individuals of

73

a certain age bracket into one bucket." She peeked up at him. "I'm working to readjust my perceptions."

He lifted her hand and nipped her knuckles. "I'll volunteer for any personal assistance you might need on that score."

"Ha." She snatched her hand free and playfully swatted his arm. "Any more personal assistance and—"

"Katie!" A woman's frantic voice rang out behind them.

A little girl with tiny pigtails and pale pink bows darted beside Zade, headed straight for the busy line of taxis.

Zade spun, caught her at the waist, and swept her high in the air before her white-sandaled foot could step from the curb.

Her giggled shriek echoed in all directions.

"Oh, God. Thank you." The mother yanked the child from Zade's easy hold and clutched her tight. "Baby, I told you, you have to stay close to mommy. You could've been hurt."

Undaunted by her mother's lectures, the little girl beamed up at Zade, who fussed over and ogled her just as brightly. The father hustled up with a little boy in tow, and offered his thanks as well.

He'd want kids. Even if by some miracle they could make a long distance relationship work, kids were something she couldn't give him. Not this late in life. Technically, she could make it happen, but realistically, she'd barely made it through the two she'd already raised. He deserved to know that joy, and he'd make an amazing father.

He cupped the back of her neck. "Hey, it's okay. She's fine."

Damn. She'd never had a decent poker face, even with her kids. At least he'd thought she was worried over the averted tragedy instead of mooning over something she couldn't have. She forced a chuckle and adjusted her purse. "The kid is fine. I assure you, the mother's heart won't beat normally for another hour."

"Fair enough." He waved down a taxi and guided her

from the curb with his hand on the small of her back. "Ready for a pool party?"

Not really. What she really wanted was to steal him away and keep him all to herself until he left the day after tomorrow. But if she had to share him, she'd make the most of it. Honor what he'd given her by sucking every minute out of the hours they had left like they were her last. "Bring it."

CHAPTER 8

ZADE SLOUCHED DEEPER in the cushioned poolside chair and nodded absently as Devin and three of his friends knocked back beers and droned about sports. Water was sloshed up on the concrete deck, WWE quality antics were mid-flight in the shallow end, and an impromptu dance off was underway by the bar. A classic college blowout, all except the handful of them gathered round the three tables furthest from the pool.

One table over, Janie threw her head back and laughed to the heavens at something one of the older women said. A camera perfect shot. The line of her neck, lips open and eyes closed in pure joy.

Four perfect days. Outside of his royal fuck up selling the business to those cookie cutter hacks in California and the anger he'd nursed after the fact, Zade usually kept a pretty easygoing attitude. A simple life governed by the peaceful teachings of his parents, but something had always seemed missing. Not the stove burner left on kind of missing. More like the-party-can't-quite-start-yet missing.

Janie had started the party. One smile and a whole life track he hadn't even known was idle, kicked into motion.

Damn, that dress looked good on her. White, crinkled linen that hugged her curves then flared out full near her ankles so it swayed when she walked. Her skin might've been standard creamy redhead fare when she'd first gotten here, but it was a light beige now. And that hair. The best part of every night was getting his hands in it, grabbing on tight, and making sure she couldn't get her lips away from his.

"I don't know, man, what do you think?"

Shit, what was Devn talking about? Oh, right. The upcoming college season. "Hard to call. Though football's not my strength, so not sure my opinion's worth much."

The music switched to something straight up pop. All the girls around Janie surged to their feet with wild shrieks and darted to the dance floor, beer in hand.

Janie bit her lip and watched them go.

God, he wished she'd join them. She'd been doing so well. Opening up, letting her emotional hair down, and laughing all the time. He loved her laugh. Throaty and deep. Kind of like when she came with his cock buried to the hilt, except then it was more of a growl.

She meandered over, hips swaying, and pulled a chair up next to him. "Is it safe over here? Or should I stay over at the girls' table?"

"Babe, you go wherever the hell you want to go." He snatched her by the wrist before she could sit and pulled her onto his lap. He lowered his voice so only she could hear. "But if you're coming over here, I want that fine ass where I can feel it."

"Ha." She kissed his forehead and her hair fell forward the same way as when she'd ridden him the night before. Her honey and vanilla perfume wrapped around him, soft as the ocean breeze at his back. "Give it five minutes and you'll be singing a different tune when your foot falls asleep from all the weight."

A few of the men cast none-to-subtle glances in their direction. They'd done it all night, most aimed on her killer curves. Every now and then he had to curb the urge to punch the bastards and tell them to mind their own damned business. Most of the time he gloated.

Cupping the back of her neck, he nipped her earlobe. "You know you could dance if you wanted. Hell, you could strip if you wanted. Pretty sure we're the only two here who'd pass a sobriety test."

"Arlo could pass."

"Yeah, but Arlo's busy selling booze and his hips don't look like yours. Got no interest in seeing him dance."

"I might do it." She cocked her head and watched the girls on the pseudo dance floor go to town. "Assuming you get me another wine and the right song comes on."

"Deal. One dance-inducing wine and a troll through Arlo's playlists." He urged her to her feet and dropped a lingering kiss to her lips. "Go easy on the boys while I'm gone. Half of them are trying to figure out how to cock block me so they can have a chance at you."

She dipped her chin and arched an eyebrow at him in disbelief as he ambled off.

Silly woman. She still didn't get it.

Shit. Maybe encouraging her to dance was a bad thing. He could buy her a drink, make some excuse to the guys about needing to leave, and take his time with her getting back to the bungalow. Not one of the men would blame him for ditching.

No, they couldn't bail yet. She wanted to dance. Had bobbed her head or tapped her foot to whatever blared out of the sound system since they'd gotten there. The bit about waiting for the right song was an excuse. A way to bide her time and build her courage. If she wanted to dance, he'd by God listen to Devin and his cronies' sports shit until she got her groove on. "Yo, Arlo."

His uncle finished two something-and-cokes and handed them off to the waiting women. He waited until they were out of earshot and muttered under his breath, "Something tells me housekeeping tomorrow is going to take twice as long."

"True, but it's their last night here and you've covered your August with their mess."

Not waiting for direction, Arlo pulled the tap on a Modelo for Zade. "Janie want something?"

"She's doing wine tonight. White."

Arlo nodded and grabbed an open bottle from the fridge beneath the counter. "She seems happy. Come to think of it, you're pretty mellow too."

Hell, yeah, he was happy. Happy and hoping he'd find a way to keep things moving with her when he got home. Assuming she could get over the age thing. The last thing he wanted was a relationship where they couldn't be themselves. "One day at a time. And don't go spouting off to Dahlia, either. She'll call mom, and that's a whole level of pressure neither one of us needs."

"Like Dahlia's not already clued in to things more than you are." Arlo handed over the drinks and turned to take the order of a dripping couple on the other side of the bar.

The Sight. Unbelievable as it sounded, his aunt did seem tuned into something pretty amazing in the way of reading how things would go down with people. He'd rather not know the answers in advance and trust his own inner voice to guide the way.

"Hold up." Zade motioned at the iPhone plugged into the sound system below the counter. "You got anything Janie would like to dance to on that thing?"

"Like what?"

"I dunno." Crap, what would she want to hear? "You got anything funky or old-school?"

Arlo smiled big enough, his slightly crooked front teeth peeked out from beneath his bushy mustache. "I think I might have something our girl would like."

Sidestepping a fat puddle on the concrete, Zade padded back to their table. There had to be a way to broach seeing her again when they got home. First things first, though. He'd have to clue her in to them practically being neighbors.

Janie sat on the edge of his chair, forearms crossed on the table and fully engaged in the conversation. Actually, she talked, they listened. Every damned one of them was focused on her like she'd drop the secret to a perfect fantasy football season in the next second.

Deep laughter rumbled around the table as he walked up.

Janie blasted him with a huge smile he felt down to his toes and stood to give him his seat.

"You didn't mention your woman's into sports," Devin said.

"I wouldn't say I'm into it." Janie took the wine and settled back on his lap, draping an arm around him. "I'd say I've had a lot of exposure to opinions. My son's a rabid football lover."

The comment tripped something in Devin's expression, like two and two had snapped together to form a winning lottery ticket combination. His gaze slid to Zade. "Yeah, that's cool." Man speak for *you lucky fucking bastard.*

Great. Now Devin and his merry band of testosterone laden sport fanatics would be hitting up thirty-plus women from here to wherever home was. Good thing tomorrow was their last day at Gypsy Cove.

A new song started up. Big horns and a funky beat he recognized but had only heard a few times.

Janie jerked upright and almost spilled her wine. "I know this one."

So did the women who'd been talking to Janie, if their happy squeals were any indication.

"My mom played this song all the time when I was growing up," Janie said. "KC & The Sunshine Band."

"The who?" Devin craned his head to watch the women

dance.

"KC & The Sunshine Band. Out of Florida." She sipped her wine and bobbed side to side. "Believe it or not, he's still touring. I bought my mom tickets to a casino show a few years ago."

Zade pulled the wine from her hand and nudged her off his lap. "There a reason you're still here?"

She hesitated, gaze trained on the other dancing girls thoroughly enjoying themselves.

He squeezed her hand. "You wanted to dance. You like the song. What's stopping you?"

She looked back at him. Her eyes brightened and her shoulders squared. "Nothing. Absolutely nothing."

And off she went.

Arlo was a fucking musical selection genius. Zade should have known she'd dance like she did everything else. Not slinky and aimed to gain men's attention, but free and full of emotion. Her head was down and her eyes were closed. She held her arms above her head, snapping and clapping every now and then, and swung her hips side to side. Sometimes she hit the beat, sometimes she didn't, but every move she made said she was one hundred percent in the moment.

"Man, you know how to pick 'em." Devin's envious voice broke through Zade's thoughts.

Pick her? He wasn't so sure about that. More like fate had offered up a chance for both of them if they were willing to face the challenges. He was damn sure willing. More than willing. He wanted more. More of her smiles. More of her no-nonsense approach to getting things done. More of the sunshine that seemed to go everywhere she went.

The song ended with a blast of horns and the girls all whooped and hollered for more.

Zade finished off his beer and stood, something primal bubbling up he didn't quite understand and didn't care to analyze. He only had two nights and one full day left to convince Janie to take that challenge with him. He'd tackle the right words for why they should be together later. Right now it was time to show her.

The song's last chord blasted through the speakers, and the crowd around Janie hooted and hollered for more. She lifted her thick hair off the back of her neck and gave a thumbs up to Arlo as half the dancers descended with demands for more from his secret playlist.

Big hands slid around her waist and splayed hip to hip. Zade. Even if she'd not grown accustomed to his citrusy cologne, she recognized him on contact. The firm press of his chest, the certainty of his touch, the electricity of his presence.

He skimmed his lips down her neck. "Is it gonna freak you out if I start carrying my camera around the rest of the time you're here?"

Tilting her head to give him and his talented mouth better access, she rested her hands on top of his and closed her eyes. The breeze cooled her heated skin and a new, slow song with a rhythm and blues feel drifted from the speakers. "Actually, I thought it was strange you hadn't already. Seems like every landscape is a postcard waiting to happen."

"I don't want it for landscapes, babe. I want it for you."

"Why?"

Those startling blue eyes of his pierced straight through to her toes. "Because when you let go, it's beautiful. Something I want to remember. Be able to look at over and over again."

Because time was almost up. Her breath hitched and a sharp pain jabbed her square in the solar plexus. She turned in his arms and threaded her fingers in his thick hair, craving the extra contact. Something to ground her equilibrium. "And what about me? Shouldn't I get some pictures to take home with me too?"

Something sparked in his eyes, so fast she almost missed it.

Almost as if she'd wounded him and challenged him all in one breath. His grin flashed bright and devious a second before he dipped and hefted her up in a fireman's carry. "I'm gonna give you a whole lot more than pictures to take home."

"Zade." With her free hand, she checked to make sure her sundress covered her butt. "Put me down. You're going to hurt yourself."

He plodded down the path to his bungalow, his gait and breathing not the least bit affected by the fact he was carting a hundred and forty-five extra pounds.

Iron Tiki Torches blazed along the way, their flames frantic in the ocean breeze. A couple close to her age strolled hand in hand toward the main resort area, their wide gazes locked on her and Zade. Well, she thought they were close to her age. It was hard to tell through her hair swinging in and out of her line of sight.

She laughed and waved. "Nothing to worry about. Just a little enthusiastic and out of control."

Zade smacked her butt.

"Ack!"

The couple cast a quick glance back in their direction and quickened their steps.

Heat from Zade's palm soothed the sting he'd left behind. "Enthusiastic, huh?"

"Well, they looked like they were ready to call the police," she said.

"They've been staying at Gypsy Cove all week, babe. They probably thought we were on our way to an orgy." He stomped up the steps to the bungalow and ducked inside, careful to watch her head. Barely pausing to click on a table lamp, he strode to the bedroom and playfully tossed her to the bed.

Her breath huffed out on a startled laugh and her hair spilled over her face. "Well." She shoved the wild mess out of her eyes and froze.

Zade stood at the foot of the bed, his button down already tossed aside and his khakis sliding past his hips. The lamp cast a muted glow behind him, outlining his muscular form in perfect definition.

"I take it we're skipping foreplay?" She'd meant it to sound mischievous, but it came out closer to Lauren Bacall demanding dessert. Which made sense. Everything about his physique made a woman want to indulge. To touch, taste, and explore every taut expanse and delectable ridge.

He tossed his black boxer briefs to join the rest of the hastily built clothes pile and straightened.

Amazing. A man no breathing woman would pass by without a second glance, no matter their sexual orientation. He was a living work of art.

He rubbed the heel of his hand above his heart. Four days she'd spent with him, and she still hadn't figured out what it meant. It was so absentminded, so reflexive in appearance, she wasn't sure he realized he did it. "See something you like?"

Everything. More than his body. She liked him. His thoughtfulness. The way he'd encouraged her to open up. To consider a life beyond what was expected and lose control. Could she do the same for him?

He planted a knee on the bed to join her.

She scrambled upright and stopped him with a palm to his chest. Urging him back a few steps, she stood before him and stroked the space above his heart. "I see something I like very much."

"I'm all yours. Whatever you want." His powerful hands settled on her hips. Firm, but careful. Cautious.

"Whatever I want?"

"Anything."

Her heart stumbled and her hands trembled. She could do this. No, she wasn't young and defying gravity in all the right places, but she was still sexy. Mature and wise. Zade had shown her that. She caressed his defined pecs and circled his dark nipples. "I thought we could change things up."

"Do I still get to strip you and find all the right spots to make you dance in bed?"

Pressing against him, she kissed his sternum and breathed in his scent. Dominant, and yet welcoming. An olfactory promise of the primitive beast trapped inside. "Maybe in a little bit. I thought I'd explore a little first."

"Not sure I like that plan as much as mine."

She swayed her hips side to side, teasing his cock with her skirt's soft linen. "Then you shouldn't have gotten undressed."

His hands tightened and a low rumble bubbled up his throat. "A good dance always turn you this naughty?"

"I don't know. I can't remember the last time I danced." Slowly, she dropped to her knees, dragging her palms down his torso, ghosting across the V at his hips, and resting them against his powerful thighs. With her lips only an inch or two from his straining erection, she let out a shaky breath.

His cock jerked and the muscles in his legs flexed. "Janie?"

"Yeah?" She nuzzled the base of his shaft and his tight sac, shaved and smooth for her lips and tongue to roam.

"Wanted to take care of you, babe."

She licked him from root to tip in small teasing flicks. "Mmm. Hmm."

"Makin' that kind of hard."

Oh, he was way past hard. Stone was more like it. Thick, hot stone. "I know. Feels great too."

"Janie, look at me."

Her pulse leapt from a jog to a sprint and the subtle swoosh of the ocean roared in her ears. The deepest intimacy. One stare to another. She circled the tip of his shaft, lifted her gaze, and sucked him deep.

"Daaamn." He gripped either side of her head. "Janie. Babe." He thrust into her mouth, stretching her lips. "Supposed to be about you." Another thrust, and his voice cracked. "Make you want more."

She cupped his balls and dragged her lips up and down his slick shaft. "You want me to let go. Be as wild as I want?" She licked the ridge on the underside, her breathing short and fast.

"Fuck yes. I told you, everything you want. Anything."

"Then I want you to let go too. No more careful."

"Janie…." It was almost a plea. So ragged she almost balked. "Don't want to scare you off."

No. He needed this. How she knew wasn't all that clear, but she felt it as firmly as a shove between her shoulder blades. She stood and eased out of reach. "Fair is fair. If I let go, you do too. No more drawing me out without you being fully on board."

One blink, and his whole demeanor shifted. A tempted, careful man one second, and an offended primal male the next. "You think I'm not on board?"

"Not all the way, no. I think you're careful with me. Afraid I'll chicken out and spend the rest of our time hiding from you."

Good Lord, his gaze could melt butter, dangerous intent radiating laser sharp on her and her alone. He stalked toward her, and her insides dipped and swirled to rival a runaway roller coaster. "Oh, I'm on board. More on board than you know."

Janie backed away, fighting the almost gravitational pull toward him.

He stroked his shaft, not letting her gain any distance. "You want it all?"

Her back hit the wall. "Yes." Maybe. With the fire in his eyes and the dangerous, almost feral cut of his jaw, she wasn't sure she'd be able to keep up. "No holds barred. Everything you've got."

He caged her with hands at either side of her head. "You gonna run?"

"No." Too fast of an answer for her common sense, but her libido purred.

He skimmed his lips along her jawline and the purr jumped to a rumble, nerve endings sparking with each touch. Hunger emanated off him, his voice tight and his chest heaving. "You'll tell me. If it's too much—"

"Zade."

"Yeah."

"Shut up and fuck me."

He growled and seized her mouth, lips slanting across hers, fingers buried deep in her hair and holding her firm for his attack. His tongue plundered, powerful stabs that matched the wicked friction of his cock against the fabric on her belly. Gone was the tender, careful lover, replaced with brutal, desperate need. An animal off its leash and mindless of anything but prurient instinct.

Dragging his teeth across her lower lip, he yanked her sundress to her waist. "Love your breasts." He cupped them, plumping them with an urgent, almost anguished clasp. He flicked his tongue against one tight peak. "Love these pretty nipples." Another flick, his fingers toying with the other. "Look like raspberries after I suck on them." He circled the tip and his hot breath fanned out along her skin. "You want that?"

She whimpered and arched closer. Torture. The way he used his lips. The things he said. Pure torture.

He drew her into his mouth and suckled deep.

A dark, uncompromising sensation speared straight between her legs. His cheeks hollowed with each merciless pull, and his soft moans oscillated along her sensitive flesh. Such a wanton and yet beautiful image, flammable fuel for an explosive lust. She'd never recover from this. Wasn't sure she wanted to.

He pulled away and studied his work, thumbing the reddened tip. "Oh, yeah. Fucking love raspberries." He licked his lower lip and went to work on its mate. The heat of his mouth scorched her delicate skin even as the breeze-cooled room teased the slick and tortured one he'd left behind.

Slipping his hand down the front of her dress and under her panties, he cupped her mound. His lips slipped from her nipple with a muted pop, and he groaned. "So wet." Back and forth, he worked the slickness between her folds, pressing his sweat-dampened forehead on hers. "You ready for me?"

"Yes."

"You sure?"

"Yes!"

He plunged two fingers deep.

Janie cried out, prying her eyes open as her sundress slipped past her hips.

"That's it, babe. Ride my fingers." With slow, purposeful strokes, he worked her. Over and over, the heel of his hand caught her clit. "Want you close, ready to go over before I give you my cock."

"Oh, God." A tremor rattled her from the inside out. The mix of his words and the raw image of his glistening fingers pumping in and out of her nearly knocked her off her feet.

"You like to watch as much as I do, don't you?" He hit his knees, jerked her panties down, and locked his gaze with hers. He licked his lower lip.

She more than liked it. She craved it. Seeing him there, on his knees, with his sinful mouth so close to her mound sent quivers through her core and feminine powering surging through her veins.

Gripping her hip with one hand and the back of her thigh with the other, he lifted one leg high and exposed her aching sex. His eyes gleamed with a predatory confidence and the fire in her blood whipped to a whole new level. "You gonna watch me eat you? Grind your pussy against my mouth?"

"Zade." She grappled for something to hold on to, nails scratching against the rough stucco walls. Anything to support her shaking legs.

"You wanted it all." He kissed the top of her mound, the brush of his lips tickling her tightly trimmed curls. His voice rumbled against her ready flesh. "Gonna let it all out and make it so you can't forget a minute."

He attacked. Feasted on her with long, devious licks, teasing her entrance with his tongue and growling against her swollen labia. His head bobbed and circled, angling to gather every last drop. Hungry. Wild and untamed.

Her belly fluttered and her sex spasmed against his tongue. He was right. She did like to watch. Was enthralled by her wetness coating his full lips and the animalistic intimacy. This was passion. Raw and wanton, and yet so indescribably pure it bathed her soul in flames.

He tongued her clit, purposeful circles and quick flicks that made the bundle of nerves ache and her thighs clench. He blew on the throbbing nub. "Brace, babe. Time for you to go up."

He closed his lips around her and sucked.

Sweet Jesus.

Slick, wet, heat. Perfect pressure. Decadent lashes from his tongue, over and over again. She needed more. The fierce, full stretch. The completeness that came every time he filled her.

The pressure intensified.

Release danced just out of reach, and her standing leg quaked. She gripped his hair at the roots and urged his mouth harder against her grinding hips. Lewd and dirty. Carnal and savage. And she didn't care. Liked it. The freedom. The power. The glory of the two of them together. "Zade, now."

His tongue darted back to her entrance.

"Zade."

"Mmmm."

"Zade, please."

More flicks against her clit, so fast she felt them like a live wire. "Louder."

"Zade!"

He shot to his feet and took her mouth, keeping her leg

anchored high and her core exposed. His iron cock dragged across her sensitized clit. "Fuck. Need a condom." He undulated against her again. "Just…" Another press, and his eyes squeezed shut. "Oh, damn, just hang on."

"Wait." Janie dug her nails into his shoulders and hung on tight. She rubbed her hips against him as best she could, keeping the delicious friction. "Can we—"

Oh, this was a bad idea. She'd warned her kids. Told them never to go unprotected. She tightened her leg wrapped around his hip and dug her heel in his flank, rolling her cleft against him while her conscience and lust wrestled. Was she really going to do this?

Heck yes, she was. Zade didn't sleep with just anyone. He was too conscientious. Too honest. And if she only had two nights left, she didn't want anything between them.

"I can't get pregnant. I had my tubes tied years ago." Her breaths came fast and furious, the burgeoning need to have him inside her, filling her until she couldn't breathe driving all her instincts. "I'm clean. I had myself tested after Gerald —"

He thrust against her, nudging her at just the right angle.

Delicious sparks of pleasure shot out in all directions, and her surprised shout echoed through the room.

"You want me bare?"

Something in his voice pried her heavy eyelids open. His expression matched his tone. Confusion. Or maybe awe.

"We don't have to," she said. "I know it's bad—"

"Yes." Determined. A caveman who'd found something he wanted and wasn't giving it up for anyone. His hips gathered steam and the muscles in his abdomen flexed and released in a glorious display of flesh. "Hell, yes." Adjusting his hips, he slicked his glans through her folds. "Want to feel you. Nothing between us."

"Nothing."

"Nothing," he whispered and speared deep.

A broken gasp scraped free, the back of her head torqued

bruisingly against the unforgiving wall. Perfect. Hard and hot. Every vein along his shaft an erotic stroke, his velvet length pistoning until she couldn't breathe. Didn't want to.

He planted the hand at her thigh against the wall, her knee hooked over his forearm. He rasped a ragged command. "Grip my neck."

Anything. Anything at all, if he kept the pace. Kept the rhythm that matched her frantic pulse. The pounding need between her legs.

He dipped, caught her standing leg on his other forearm, and pushed back up, bracing both hands on the wall.

Oh, dear God, he was deep. So amazingly buried inside her, the sensation stole her breath. Her back was wedged against the wall, legs splayed wide and at the mercy of his ruthless hips. Erotic and untamed.

And the sounds. She could come just from the sound of Zade's sexy groans and heavy breaths at her ear. The slick, wet shuttle of his cock. The slap of skin against skin, and the decadent rap of his balls with each assault.

He lifted his chest and watched his shaft tunnel deep. "Look at us."

She couldn't. Her release was too close, and for once in her life she didn't want the sex to end. It couldn't. Not yet.

"Look at us, Janie."

His thick cock. Veins stark against pink flesh. Stretching her. Filling her in the most perfect way.

"Who's inside you?"

She snapped her head up.

"Who?" he demanded. "Who's fucking you?"

"You."

"Me." He deepened his strokes and her breath caught. "Us. Perfect. Just. Like. This."

He pounded harder, relentless and savage. "Take it, babe. Wanna feel you milk me with nothing between us." He rammed once, twice, three and—

"Yes!" Her pussy clenched slow and fierce around his cock,

and a deep, throbbing wave ricocheted out across her body.

Zade growled in her ear. "Fuck, Janie." He stabbed deep. "God, yes." His shout rang out and his cock jerked inside her, hard flexes that fired tiny shocks up her spine.

Pulse after pulse. Spasm after spasm. Delicious quakes rattling through her core and heaving feeble cries past her throat. So powerful. The bite of an unseen brand on her heart, and a memory seared in her mind. One to cling to when reality swept her under.

Her heart tripped and she tightened her arms around his neck.

No. Reality wasn't here yet. They still had the rest of the night and another full day. This was their time. Reality couldn't rob her of it. Not yet.

Zade rested his forehead on hers, his eyes closed and breathing heavy. His arms were still braced against the wall, the muscles bunched tight as stone. He chuckled, irony or disbelief tempering the sound of it. "Thought the whole little death thing was bullshit." He kissed her, a slow, easy press of lips that lingered in a way more powerful than words. "I was wrong."

He gently slid one arm out from underneath her leg and guided it around his waist. Clutching her torso tight to his, he repeated the process with the other. "You okay?"

Entirely the wrong word. Not even in the right neighborhood. Dumbfounded, maybe. Altered. Poised for a heartbreak that made her divorce look pale. None of which she could tell him. "I think I've worked off dinner and half of lunch."

A slow, deep laugh rumbled through him as he carried her to the bed, his cock still buried inside her. "Is that all?" He laid them so they stretched tangled in the center of the pristine white sheets. "Oh, wait. I forgot. It was me doing the heavy lifting."

She palmed his sweat-slicked arms and shoulders. Never for the rest of her life would she forget the feel of him. The way his muscles flexed, holding her defenseless to his carnal assault. "You're young and able. We older folk need to be looked after in our doddering years."

He rolled his hips. A slow, leisurely glide that spoke of deep, erotic intimacy. His eyes were intense, saying something she couldn't quite grasp, but resonated clear to her soul. "I like looking out for you."

And she wanted more. Damn it, it wasn't fair. A man who made her feel alive, the first to make her chase passion instead of reason, and he lived thousands of miles away.

He eased away and his softening length slipped free. Sitting back on his heels, he ran his hand along his semi-erect shaft and rubbed their mixed essence between his fingers. The playful expression of moments before altered, morphing to a face so serious and thoughtful, her instincts pricked to attention.

"Zade?"

He gently urged her knees apart and slicked his fingers through her sex. So many emotions passed across his face, not one of them easily identifiable. But they were deep. Almost tangible in the tense silence.

He circled her entrance. "My first time."

Goose bumps scattered across her sweat dampened skin. "What?"

He splayed his hand atop her abdomen, the span so wide he nearly touched each hipbone. His gaze was locked on the space beneath his palm and his voice came out graveled and awed. "Never let myself come inside a woman before."

Oh, my God. The confession shook her. Rattled something so fundamental it threatened to free and break her all in one pass. "Zade, I didn't know. I shouldn't—"

"I'm glad it was you. I wouldn't trade it. Not for a second." He cupped her hips and pressed a reverent kiss to the space above her belly button. "Thank you."

He was thanking her. Acting like she'd gifted him with the priceless gift of her virginity when she'd been the one doing all the taking. She speared her fingers into his hair, the need to comfort and protect so powerful, she almost roared to the ceiling. "Zade," she whispered instead.

Turning his head, he rested the side of his face above the space he'd kissed and stretched out between her legs, arms hugging her hips.

The urge to speak battered her, pushing to ease the tension, but nothing came. Nothing seemed worthy of his bared emotion. Of his passion and care.

She sifted her fingers through hair and settled into his peaceful presence. No, she couldn't say anything. There weren't words meaningful enough to convey what she felt. But she could show him. For twenty-four more hours, she could give him everything she had. She'd mend the damage losing him would do her heart when he was gone.

CHAPTER 9

HER HAIR WASN'T auburn. For thirty minutes while Janie slept, Zade had sat in the bedside chair, studying the sunlight glinting off her hair. He'd thought it was auburn, but he was wrong. It was cinnamon, just enough chestnut mixed in with the copper and amber threads to make the unique, rich color.

God, he sounded like a girl. He propped his elbows on his knees and fisted his hair with both hands on the top of his head. Yeah, photography had given him a more than intimate knowledge of colors through the years, but he'd never hovered bedside over a woman and tried to nail her hair color. What the hell was wrong with him?

You want more and you don't want to lose her.

A stark, clear statement straight from the universe. The kind so bold and powerful it slapped him silly and dared him not to listen.

He rubbed his sternum, willing, almost begging for more. How to broach the topic. How to admit he'd sidestepped clarifying where he lived and why. Two sizable land mines he had no idea how to navigate without blowing his heart into tiny chunks.

Beneath the tangled sheets, Janie rolled to her side facing him and pulled in a slow, sexy breath. A pillow was tucked to her side and her arm was crooked around it with her hand resting near her mouth. That hair. That wild, tangle-your-hands-in-me-and-see-what-it-gets-you cinnamon colored hair splayed out against the crisp white sheets. Naturally sexy.

Her eyelids lifted, relaxed and drowsy. "Hey."

"Hey." Way to start off smart. Hit her with some college he-man language. Fuck, he was gonna blow this.

"Your eyebrows kind of wing up at the ends when you're angry." Her voice was hushed, the same intimate tone she'd used with him before they'd fallen asleep last night, naked and tangled chest to toes. "They didn't look that way before we went to sleep. Something happen with your business?"

"What makes you say that?"

"Because the only time I've seen you angry is when you're thinking about your bad business deal."

Or when he was thinking about how not to fuck up something else good. "I'm not angry."

"Wanna talk about it?"

He clasped his hands between his widened legs. He'd been direct with her so far; maybe that was the way to go. A rip-the-Band-aid approach. If it didn't work, he could sex her into oblivion again and try something else. He opened his mouth.

Make her see.

He closed his mouth.

Make her see what you see.

His heart shook off its languid beat and stretched for action. She was visual, just like him. If she could see what he saw, surely she'd get it. Be willing to risk time together in the real world. "I want to ask you for something."

She shifted to push herself upright.

"No." He shot forward and stopped her. "Don't move."

Her muscles uncoiled beneath his palm and she eased back to the bed. "Okay." Her tension might have been gone, but the sun sparked off her hazel eyes and called out her wariness. "What do you want?"

He sat back down. "I want to take your picture."

She blinked a few times. "Me?"

"You. I want you to see through my eyes. Right where you are. Right now."

Her gaze flitted across the bed, the length of her body, the open skylight.

"Nothing lewd, I promise." There had to be something to say. A nudge to get her over the hump. "I need this."

She stared at him for long seconds.

He fisted one hand and squeezed it with the other. Maybe showing her with pictures was too much. He'd go the sexual oblivion route and come up with something—

"Okay."

His heart stopped then jolted back into rhythm. "Okay?"

She nodded, a cautious, tiny dip of her chin that showed how carefully he'd have to tread.

"Okay." Relief. Sweet fucking relief. He stood and rubbed his hands together, feet itching to move. "Stay right there. Let me get my camera."

"Are you going to put any clothes on?"

"Why? You're naked. Besides, looking at you gives me a semi, so I'd just have to take my clothes off again when we're done." He rummaged through the bottom dresser drawer, and the sheets rustled behind him. "Don't move."

Her giggle floated down to him. "It was my legs. Surely I can wiggle a little."

"You wiggle a lot while you sleep." He prepped in smooth practiced movements, a second-nature checklist clicking through his head. Surprising, considering the adrenaline blasting through his bloodstream.

"Are you complaining?"

"Never." He turned and froze. He'd paid so damned much attention to her face and the sexy arch of her lips, he hadn't stopped to consider this angle. The sheet draped from the highest curve of her hip to just above her perfect ass, and her hair fell in tight, waterfall waves across her shoulders.

Light. Focus. Shoot.

The camera whirred and her muscles clenched. "Zade?"

"It's okay." His voice rumbled a half-octave lower than normal. "Your hips are beautiful." Click. "The line of your spine makes me want to touch you. The way the sheet's wrapped around you makes me want to dip my hand beneath it and explore."

Her head shifted enough to bring her elegant profile into the picture, her eyes downcast and wary. "Is that how you draw the women in your photos out? Tell them what you see?"

He rounded the foot of the bed, camera lowered. "Have I told them they're beautiful? Absolutely. But I've never crossed the line and told them I wanted contact because it's never happened. To get the truth out of them, to draw them out, they have to have the truth from me."

She bit her lip, and he whipped the camera into place on reflex.

Click.

Too late. Her gaze was glued to the bed, the raw expression shuttered. "Need you to look at me, Janie. Look past the camera. See me. Forget it's there and focus on me."

Her fingers smoothed back and forth on the pillow near her face. "I feel a little self-conscious."

"You didn't feel self-conscious last night."

A crooked smile. Pretty white teeth. Head tilted and eyes glazed. Perfect.

Click.

Her gaze whipped to the camera, and the smile slipped.

"Look through it, babe. I'm right here." He kept the camera in place and shifted his angle, bracing a knee on the bed. "I mentioned trust, yeah?"

She nodded, some of her wariness slipping away.

"I'd never lie to you, but I could have cleared something up the first day we went sailing. I was afraid to point out something you'd misunderstood because I thought it would give you a chance to run."

She cocked her head, and a lock of hair fell across her chest, dipping into the valley between her breasts.

Click. Click.

"I don't live in California. That's only where the company that bought my business is from."

"Oh." She pursed her mouth and her gaze slid sideways. "Then where are you from?"

Focus, check. "I've got a condo in Uptown Dallas."

Wide eyes. Surprise. A quick flush on her cheeks and across her collarbone and so much longing, it moved something inside him.

Hope.

Click. Click. Click.

He lowered the camera. It was still there. Guarded, but still there, brightening her hazel eyes so they bordered on pale teal. He checked the last three shots. Yep. Even on the tiny screen he could see it. And if he could see it, so could she.

That was it. The key.

He lifted the camera back into place. "I thought you'd be angry."

She opened her mouth, shut it, and opened it again. "I can't." Her gaze drifted to the sheets.

"Eyes to me, babe."

A scowl marred the spot between her eyebrows. "You should have told me."

"I should have. But you're not mad?"

One corner of her mouth quirked. "No."

"Why not?"

Such a pretty smile. Easy and accepting. "Because you're

right. I would've run."

"But you wouldn't run now?"

Her smile slipped and her lips parted. "No."

Click.

"Roll over on your stomach." God, he hoped this worked. If it didn't, even weeks of sexual oblivion wouldn't be enough to give him another chance.

She studied him, the energy around her shifting to something sharp and cautious, but pushed the pillow out of her way and shifted so her arms were crooked above her head. "Like this?"

"Almost." He kneeled on the bed, keeping a forty-five degree angle on the line of her body. "Now push back on your hands and knees."

She stayed completely still, her voice little more than a whisper. "Zade."

He lifted the camera. "Can you trust me, Janie?"

The only movement was the slow, minuscule rise of her shoulders with each breath.

A painful, razor-lined fist seemed to grip his heart, and he fought to keep the shot free of the fear shaking his hands.

Slowly, she slid her hands to either side of her chest, palms whispering across the smooth sheets. Her hair fell in a heavy wave and covered her face. "I trust you."

Power blasted through him, a rush headier than the one bungee jump he'd dared in college and ten times as addictive. "Thank you." It seemed a lame thing to say, but necessary. An acknowledgement of her gift.

"What now?"

Shit. He needed his head in the game or he'd fuck this whole thing up. "Sweep your hair over to one side so I can see the line of your neck. That's it. Just like that."

"I don't think I can look at the camera like this."

"It's okay. It's fine like this for now." Hell, it was better. He'd get her eyes when the time was right. "Right now I want you to think. Close your eyes and imagine my lips on your shoulder."

Her head tipped back an inch, and her lips parted on a small inhalation.

Click.

"Where do you want them now?" he said.

She angled her head to one side, practically drawing him a map. "My neck."

He chuckled, snapping random shots with each subtle shift. "Remember what I said about your spine?"

"Mmm hmm."

Fighting back his groan nearly cost him his tongue. He loved that husky, floating voice of hers. How she seemed to let go and get lost in the moment. Watching it was even better. "If I were behind you right now, I'd urge your knees further apart, cover your back and work my lips down every inch of it."

She groaned and pushed back, angling her hips up and stretching her arms out in front of her.

Jesus, God Almighty, he was gonna come from the visual alone. She was in the moment. Now was the time for the shot. "Janie?"

"Mmmm."

"There's nothing I like more than touching you." He snapped shots at will. "Making you feel good. Tasting you. Hearing the little noises you make." He paused, letting her ride whatever thoughts and scenarios were in her head. "Look at me, babe. Let me see your eyes."

She gazed over one shoulder, eyelids heavy with passion.

He focused on the elegant angle of her jaw and the delicate curve of her shoulder. "I don't want this to end. I want to let this play out when we get home. Feel more. Grow more."

Click. Click. Click. Click.

Fear. Need. Longing. Hope. They all played out for the camera, raw and so blatant, he felt them like a knife.

He tossed the camera to the bed and nudged her knees

wide, like he'd promised. "You want it too." He kissed the spot she liked where her neck and shoulder met and worked his way toward her spine. "I saw it, Janie."

"It's not that simple."

"It's as simple as we make it." He pulled her hips to his and sat back on his heels, pulling her upright, her back to his front. He skimmed her rib cage. Teased the sensitive undersides of her breasts. "I like making you laugh. Talking to you. Sleeping next to you, even when you wiggle. We can have that. More. See where it goes."

Her head dropped forward. "I can't have kids. Even if I physically could, I don't think I'd be up for it emotionally."

Kids. Jesus, he hadn't even thought of that. But didn't the fact that he'd never so much as imagined normal family life say something in itself?

"Babe." He guided her chin to where he could watch her face. "Some guys want the text book, but that's not me. I've never once imagined myself with a nine to five and two point five prescribed kids. I want to explore. Live. See things. If I want to share love with a kid, there are a shit ton of ways I can do that without my woman getting pregnant."

She gasped and her nails bit into his thighs. "You can't mean that."

"Do I strike you as the average guy?"

"No." Oh, those big eyes. So cute. Guileless and sincere. He liked them heavy with lust better.

He slid his hand up her inner thigh. "Does that mean you're going to agree and let us see where this goes?"

"I need…" She swallowed and widened her knees, eyes sliding shut. "I need to think about it."

"Hmmm." He teased the tight curls above her pussy. "Thought we'd established thinking's overrated. Go with your gut. What's it say?"

"It says you're a devious strategist with wicked fingers and a beautiful voice."

The woman was out of her fucking mind. His voice wasn't

beautiful, hers was. Throaty and made for tempting men until they groveled. He rubbed his cheek against hers, his morning stubble reddening her creamy skin. "Then you know it's best to agree now and save yourself the trouble."

"Zade." She wiggled her ass against his aching cock and gripped his wrists. "Talk later. Touch now."

"Bossy." He dipped his finger between her legs, tracing the seam where her inner thigh met her core. "Say yes and I'll give you what you want."

She dug her head into his shoulder, arching her neck and back so her perfect tits begged for attention.

He teased the delicate tip of one with his free hand, circling the tight nipple. "Say it, babe. At least tell me you'll think about it."

"Okay."

Quick. Too quick. He pressed his cock against her ass. "Seriously, Janie. No lip service. You admit you want this, and we'll talk it out."

She covered his hand at her breast with hers and urged him to squeeze the tight mound. "Yes. Seriously." She cupped the other neglected breast and opened her eyes, gaze lingering on the sensual image. "Please. Now."

Hell, yes.

He gave her what she wanted, priming her with his fingers and tweaking her nipple in the same rhythm. "This is right. Swear to God, Janie. It's perfect."

She leaned forward, planting her hands in the mattress and offering her pretty pink pussy in the most delectable pose ever.

He splayed his hand at the small of her back, deepening the arch. "Need my cock?"

"Yes."

His dick jerked in agreement and his thighs clenched. He lined himself up, savoring her smooth ass. "Gonna remind you how perfect this is. Make sure you can't forget."

He rammed home and her head whipped back, her hair

spilling across her back like fire. Heat engulfed him, her moist, tight channel trembling around his aching shaft to the point he thought he'd lose his fucking sight. God, this woman was special. His. For how long he didn't know, but fuck, he was gonna hang on as long as he could.

He shuttled deep, hands clasped at her hips, skin slapping against skin, and dirty, animalistic sounds rumbling around them. "Hands between your legs. Finger that sweet clit and bring us both off."

She moaned and answered with quick, nimble circles.

"That's it," he whispered. Almost there. Her pussy tightened and he angled downward, nudging the spot along her front wall. His balls were high and taut. Ready. So damned ready. "Come on, Janie. Give me—"

Her shout rang out and her sex fisted him in a brutal grip, scalding contractions that undulated up and down his shaft.

Every muscle wrenched tight and pleasure speared from his groin to the ends of hair. His cock jerked and flexed inside her, filling her. Marking her. Claiming her.

His.

He covered her back with his chest, hips rocking against hers as they leveled off. Their skin was slippery with sweat and her heartbeat reverberated in a rhythm similar to his. He cupped her mound and reveled in the slick glide of his release against her swollen lips. She couldn't change her mind. He wouldn't let her. No way was he letting her run.

CHAPTER 10

JANIE WIGGLED HER toes, and the dried sand from her walk along the beach with Zade crumbled to the lounger cushion. The only place bearable in the three o'clock heat was napping in an air-conditioned room, in the water, or beachside and in the shade, like she was right now.

Only one more full day before time to head home, and most of it without Zade since his flight left at some insane hour the next morning.

Funny. She'd imagined coming here, isolating herself from humanity, and making peace with the prospect of a lonely future. Now she couldn't imagine being here without Zade, didn't want the quiet, and was entertaining the exact opposite of an anticlimactic life. Destiny just kept doling out surprises.

Zade stretched in the lounger beside her and let out an indelicate man-yawn. He took advantage of the nearly non-existent space between their chairs and slid his leg closer to hers, knocking more sand to the cushion with his none-to-

105

subtle game of footsie. "Thought you were going to take a nap."

Oh, that voice. The just woken, sleep-sexy voice. Deep and a little gravelly. Intimate because the only time she heard it was first thing in the morning after snuggling with him all night. She could have more of that. Assuming she'd pull her big girl panties up long enough to glom onto it. "My mind was too busy."

"Mmmm." He rolled to his side and lifted her chair back enough to unhinge the lever propping her up.

"What are you doing?"

"Helping." He eased the top half down to match his lounger's supine position. Reaching across her, he grabbed the side of her chair and tugged so the two were flush, then wrapped her up, their legs tangled and his torso perpendicular with hers. "Figured a little anchor for those thoughts of yours might be in order."

"But what if I don't want to lie down?"

One of his arms rested across her chest, his hand idly stroking her shoulder. He slid it up toward her neck and traced her jawline with his thumb. "Then I'd find another way to anchor you. Whatever it takes."

This was what she wanted for her kids. Partners who looked out for them and weren't so strung up in their own heads, they never bothered to care for anyone else. How ironic that Zade was offering her that very thing and she couldn't seem to find the courage to dive in headfirst.

He nuzzled the side of her neck, comforting more than seductive. "You want to talk about it?"

There it was again. Thoughtful and pragmatic, not to mention off the charts sexy. If she was seriously going to consider a relationship with this man, she'd be smart to talk to him and see how well they worked through issues.

A laugh huffed out of her strong enough to jostle his arm on her chest. "Just wrapping my head around the word relationship after ending a twenty-two year marriage is challenging enough. Imagining how we'd face one as unconventional as ours has me in a mind freeze."

"So, we try it on. Talk through some scenarios." He propped himself up on an elbow and smoothed a stray lock of hair off her neck. "Shoot. Give me one."

"Okay." Didn't it figure? She'd had one thought after another ping around her head for the last hour. Now when she needed one, not a damned one poked its head up. "How about if we start on your side?"

"Like?"

"I don't know. I guess I'd like an idea of what your life is like away from here. Do you work a lot? Volunteer? Go to a lot of parties?"

"Parties?"

"Yeah." She shrugged. It seemed a silly question, now that she'd said it out loud. "Every time Thomas comes home from college he heads out to one party or another. You might have five years on him, but you're still in the same age bracket."

"I guess I get together with friends now and then, yeah."

"So what are they like?" she said. "Is it like the pool party yesterday?"

"Did it seem like my kind of scene?"

Attire and demeanor wise, no. He'd been more of a casual professional, where they'd been carefree tank tops and bikinis. He'd kept to the less boisterous tables and quite literally carted her out of the chaos as fast as he could. "No, but you were friends with them before I showed up. I assumed that might be how your life is at home."

He cocked his head and narrowed his eyes.

Seriously? How could he not get it? "You were playing football, remember? My knee, your nuts?"

He smiled wide and fast, almost as blinding as the sun flashing off the rippling water in the cove. "Babe, that was more man code, boredom, and sucking up for Arlo than my idea of a good time. Never thought I'd say I was glad a

woman busted my balls, but in this case, best accident ever."
He leaned in and brushed his lips against hers.

After another considering smile, he rolled to his back
beside her and laced his hands behind his head. "What else
you got?"

Okay. So, no crazy *Animal House* type parties on the agenda
for the near future. That was promising. And while Devin
and the rest of his pals hadn't been her cup of tea, they'd
been pretty accepting of her. Somehow she didn't see the
people in her circles being quite so understanding. Did she
really want people in her life who judged her on such a
shallow basis?

"Scares me when you pucker your mouth up like that." He
went back to playing footsie with her.

"I have no idea how the people in my life are going to
respond to the concept of me dating a younger man." She
rolled to her side. "Do you still call it dating? Is that what
we'd be doing?"

His lips lifted in a lazy, almost devious grin and his eyelids
grew heavy. "We'd be in a relationship. A monogamous one.
We'd get to know each other. Do what couples do."

"More than just sex?"

He unwound one arm and ran his knuckles up and down
her bicep. "How much of our time this week was sex?"

"Nights mostly."

"Right. I spent my days with you too. Not just to get to the
nights, but to get to you." The steady up and down of his
hand hesitated. "The first time I picked up a camera and
took a shot, a whole new dimension opened up in my life. It
was there all the time, I just didn't know it. Once I felt it, I
wanted more." He touched her cheek. "Meeting you? Same
thing."

Her stomach did a triple flip and at least half of her brain
short-circuited.

"Not gonna lie, though." His knuckles grazed the side of
her breast, a tiny gesture no one else would notice, but that

sparked all kinds of attention from the nerve endings beneath his touch. "I'm equally fond of the time when there's little to no clothing involved and I'm buried balls deep in your hot pussy."

And there went the rest of her brain, the bulk of her blood rushing to aid and abet the growing ache between her legs. "You're naughty," she whispered.

He winked and put his hand back behind his head in a pleased-with-himself posture. "Just being honest."

Her stomach grumbled embarrassingly loud.

Zade's sharp laughter rang out behind it, echoing through the cove. "Apparently, I'm giving you a workout too. We just ate three hours ago."

"Yes, but you ate enough for three of us. I ate enough for half of me and I'm still burning calories from last night."

Still laughing, but far more delicately than before, he stood and shook out his towel. "Pack up your stuff."

"What? Why?"

"Because I gotta feed my woman if she's gonna keep up until my flight leaves." He looped the towel around his neck and stepped into his flip-flops. "Besides, I wanna get those pics off my memory card and onto a flash drive before tonight. Arlo's got a computer I can use in the office. We'll stop, transfer the pictures, and grab a quick snack to bring back here."

She couldn't move. Just spun the phrase round and round in her head. She was forty-years old, for crying out loud. Not sixteen.

He took two steps toward the bungalow, stopped and backtracked. "Something wrong?"

Not wrong. Not unless she considered the fluttering fanfare in her stomach to be a bad thing. She waved him toward the room. "No, I'm great." *Liar.* "Grab your stuff and we'll head up."

The buzz from his possessive statement was still zipping through her bloodstream ten minutes later. Thank God, Arlo had fitted out the lobby with ceiling fans. No way could she fight the heat and the growing prospect of her future with Zade at the same time.

As they reached the front desk, he kissed her on the temple and unwound his fingers from hers. "Won't take five minutes. You wanna hang up here with Arlo or come with me in the office?"

Two taxis pulled into the small circular drive. Arlo dodged back and forth behind the registration desk with a healthy flush on his face, checking in a decent size party.

"I think I'm gonna need a few glasses of wine before I'm ready to see my big boudoir debut." She smoothed her hand across his chest and kissed his cheek. So normal. Like an ordinary couple. "I'll stay up here and see if I can't find a way to help your uncle. He looks a little flustered, and more just pulled up."

"He's got a secret stash of those mini-sized cokes in the fridge. You want one?" he said over his shoulder as he ambled away.

"Do you know how many calories are in those?"

He grinned and winked before he disappeared into the office.

Of course, he didn't know how many calories were in them. He was twenty-six and had a metabolism to rival a dinosaur. Though if things kept up between them, her metabolism might pick up too.

The two new sets of guests had their suitcases out in front of the taxis and were paying their drivers. Yet again, the bellboy was nonexistent.

She couldn't help Arlo much on the computer, but she could probably swing claim checks for the arriving guests' bags and see if they wanted something to drink. She strode to the bell stand and rifled through the top drawer. Claim checks and pens. Voila.

She filled in the blanks for the couples, lugged their bags off to one side, and did the loopty-loop thing with the stretch tag around the handles. "If you'd like to have a seat in the lobby, your host will be with you as soon as he's finished checking in the other guests."

Zade's voice cut across the room from behind her. "I'm almost done. I found some Gatorade, too. You want one of those?"

"No thanks, sweetie. You finish up." She refocused on the two couples and walked them to the cozy rattan seating arrangement with its teal and mango cushions. "Have you all been to Gypsy Cove before?"

"No, it's our first time," one of the women said. She was about Janie's age, maybe five years older, but had a hairstyle that made the age difference seem closer to ten or fifteen years apart. "I hear it's a little different than the other resorts."

A chuckle slipped out before she could check it. "Oh, it's different for sure. But it's lovely and the people who run it are wonderful."

The woman laid a hand over her heart and lowered her voice. "I have to tell you. Your son is very attractive. You must be proud."

"My son?"

The lady straightened from her conspiratorial posture and beamed a brilliant smile, eyes locked over Janie's shoulder.

Footsteps shuffled behind her.

Zade.

He cupped the back of her neck and pulled her around to face him. "Babe, wait 'til you see those pictures. They're amazing." He kissed her. A slow, perfect mesh of their lips, warm and intimate. Wiping away the world in one lingering touch. He eased away, his eyes heated, lifted his head and locked gazes with the people behind her. "Something wrong?"

The world unlocked from its standstill and reality sideswiped her with a replay of the woman's comment. Janie held her breath and turned.

Slack jawed. Every one of them. The woman who'd called Zade Janie's son held her hand at her throat. Her mouth hung open and she dipped her chin with a contemptible slant. "Well. I see I misunderstood. Seems things here at Gypsy Cove do run to the unexpected."

The veiled barb struck between each rib as swiftly as a dozen daggers, and her conscience beat against its temporary holding cell. This was what it would be like. Everywhere.

Janie lifted her chin and smiled, though her cheeks shook with the effort. "An innocent mistake. Don't think a thing about it. Why don't you all have a seat and make yourselves comfortable?"

Slow steady breaths. One in. One out. Her beach bag sat next to the bell stand, the yellow and white colors mocking the cloying panic in her stomach. Her room. If she could grab a minute alone she could settle her thoughts. Disassociate.

"Janie." Zade gripped her bicep.

She pulled away and hurried to her bag. Sunscreen, two novels, sunglasses.

Key.

"Janie, take it easy. They made a bad assumption."

"Everyone is going to make that assumption." Well, maybe not everyone. Anyone younger than her would probably be fine, which knocked pretty much anyone she knew out of the equation. She hustled through the lobby, painting a wide swath around the four waiting to check in.

Zade's firm strides sounded right behind hers. "Babe, we need to talk about this. You don't have to panic. It's okay."

"Did you see her face?" Her legs couldn't move any faster, not without breaking into a jog. "My God, she glared at me like I was some depraved, incestuous freak."

Almost there. Four more doors, and she could let it out. Put her head between her knees and let the tears go.

"It's her limitation. Not yours." He glanced back toward the guests waiting in the hallway and practically growled.

"Don't take that on. Don't let it rob you of something good."

The key fob jangled and slipped from her shaking hand.

Zade snatched it from the floor and held it out of reach. "Don't do this. Don't run from me. Don't run from us."

God, he was beautiful. Inside and out. A person who challenged others to be more just by being around him.

She lifted her chin toward the lobby at the far end of the hall. "What just happened? That's reality. Wrong, right, or indifferent, that's what we're going to face. Or, more accurately, what I'm going to face. I'm the one they're going to judge. She wasn't looking at you. She was looking at me. Thinking what an indecent cradle robber I am. It hurt."

"Do I want to walk away from us? No." A pained laugh ripped past her throat. "I love being with you. You make me feel alive in a way I didn't even realize was possible, but I'm going to be the one who faces that reaction, and I've got to figure out if I'm brave enough to face it."

She held out her hand for the key.

His chest rose and fell in shallow breaths and his lips pressed tight.

"Give it to me, Zade. This has to be a two way street and you've got to let me buy in on my own."

He opened his palm and stared at the key, the tension in his frame so rigid she half expected him to fling it down the hallway. "You're right. Bullying you into a relationship wouldn't bode well for either of us." He dug into his pocket, pulled something out, and laid it in his palm alongside the key.

A thumb drive. Her pictures.

"I can't tell you how to feel and I can't tell you how to act, but you can tell yourself." He held them both out to her. "See for yourself. Take a good, hard look at the woman in those pictures. See if you're willing to lose that."

She scooped them from his outstretched palm, her fingers frigid against his comforting heat.

"My taxi's coming at seven in the morning," he said. "If

you're there to see me off, we'll figure out what to do next and we'll do it together. If you're not…" He shrugged and rubbed the heel of his hand over his sternum. "I'll leave you alone."

"Zade, I'm sorry—"

"Don't." He mashed his lips together and shoved his hands in his pockets. His beautiful blue eyes sparked with icy disappointment. "You said what you needed to say, so don't apologize." He lifted his chin toward the door and walked away, his head held high. "I'll be in the lobby well before seven. Figure out what's right for you."

CHAPTER 11

OVER AND OVER, Janie tapped the plastic thumb drive on the desk in her room, slid her fingers down its length, spun it over and started again.

A bottle of opened but not yet touched merlot sat on the corner of the desk, a standard issue glass tumbler beside it, ready for action. Her laptop was open, but the screen was dark, sleep mode having kicked in way before her courage. The alarm clock on the nightstand reflected in the mirror to one side of her, the only splash of color in the otherwise dark room.

12:14 AM

Big, bold red letters that practically screamed what an idiot she was. Eight hours lost that could have been spent with Zade. Usually by this time of night she was curled up next to him and in a sexual coma.

The revulsion on the woman's face flashed front and center in Janie's memory. Pinched eyes. Accusing and judgmental.

"It's her limitation. Not yours. Don't take that on. Don't make it rob you of something good."

Twenty-six years old, and yet in many ways, Zade was so much wiser. Confident and centered in who he was.

She pulled her iPhone closer and pressed the button at the bottom. The screen blinded her with a candid picture of Mckenna and Thomas at last year's state fair. Who really mattered in this equation? Her and Zade, for sure. Her kids. Her family, to a certain degree. Not for approval, but for support. The same for his family.

With slow, thoughtful strokes, she thumbed through her contacts and pulled up Mckenna's number. All she wanted for her kids was for them to be happy. To live full, healthy lives, and experience a lifetime of love and passion, even if it came in the form of someone or something unconventional. Why couldn't she allow that for herself?

She scoffed and propped her head on her hands. Because she was afraid. Terrified, actually. Her life had been so safe. Steady and predictable.

And blank. A huge canvas with nothing of her own on it. Not one speck of color. Worse, she hadn't even realized the absence until she'd met Zade. Yes, she'd raised two wonderful children, but those were their lives. Their colors. If her world was already blank, she didn't exactly have a lot to lose.

Except Zade. The man who'd encouraged her. Who offered up different palettes for consideration. Who saw her as a woman. Who fought for her even when she wanted to run.

She opened her hand. The thumb drive lay warm in her palm, daring her to see someone new. To throw a splash of color on the canvas.

"See for yourself. Take a good, hard look at the woman in those pictures. See if you're willing to lose that."

She touched the track pad and her login popped up.

Login: JanieMcAllister

116

Password: MckennaThomas

She huffed out an ironic laugh as she punched the enter key. Even her login and password information was bland. She should change it to FixitMomma or ProblemWringer101.

Or SexyBabe4Zade.

She plugged the thumb drive in the USB and poured herself a ridiculously large glass of wine. The trick was not to think too much about it. Just pull the pictures up and assess. No big deal. Easy peasy.

There it was. A folder entitled Janie McAlister with lots of files beneath it that ended in .jpg.

The wine's berry tang burst against her tongue and her heart punched a few extra kicks of encouragement.

Click.

A picture of her facing away from the camera filled the screen. It wasn't done in black and white, but the coloring gave it a similar look and feel. She cocked her head to one side, held captive by the simple, yet elegant image. From this view, her hips looked pretty nice. Not at all the way she'd felt about them when trying on bathing suits for the trip.

She took another sip of her wine and clicked the next one. Not bad. Not bad at all.

Click. Study. Sip.

Click. Study. Sip.

Every picture drove her pulse higher. Hotter than the one before it. She had colors in these pictures. She was bold. Beautiful. Even sexy. Not bland at all.

Click.

Her nearly empty glass thunked to the desk and her breath hitched. All of a sudden the lingering wine on her tongue seemed too thick, clinging to the top of her mouth. This was the moment. He'd told her he didn't want it to end and everything inside her had cried out, "Yes."

It was right there. A message painted as bold as a three story neon sign. Simple and yet staggeringly profound. Was she willing to let something that moved her this much go simply based on the opinions of strangers?

No.

She grinned and imagined Zade beside her, adding an enthusiastic, "Hell, no." to the mix. It said something, her thinking of him in this moment. Feeling him here even when he was in a completely different building. If she was smart, she'd rectify that situation and make it so they were in the same bed.

Shutting the laptop, she gulped down what was left of her wine and poured herself another celebratory glass. She could do this. She could not only do it, she could own it. Set a good example for her kids. For her daughter.

Shoot. She needed to call Mckenna and Thomas and give them a heads up. At least that way they'd have a day to assimilate the news and gather their thoughts. She could sit down with them when she got home and let them drill her with questions.

She plunked back down, nearly missing the chair altogether and only landing one half of her butt cheek on the seat. Wine always went to her head, but this round had taken the loopy express.

Oh, yeah. She hadn't eaten. That made sense.

Not a problem. She'd call Mckenna first and jot over to the dining hall for a snack.

Glass in hand, she dialed up her youngest and relocated to the bed. She should have napped with Zade today and given her mind a rest. If she had, she'd have been able to process the run-in with the judgmental lady in the lobby with a little more class and a lot less drama.

God, she hoped Zade wasn't too angry. She sipped her wine and waited for Mckenna to pick up. Surely he'd understand. She'd have to be sure and let him know she wasn't going to waffle on him. That she'd decided to make a go of this thing between them and only toss in the towel when they both agreed it wasn't working. Not when a complete stranger said it was wrong.

"Mom!"

Ah, Mckenna. So full of life and happy. Ready to tackle the world. "Hey, sweetie. I know it's late. I hope I didn't wake you up."

"Nope. Just got home from a movie with Jessica. How's Mexico? You ready to come home?"

Hardly. "Actually, I'm having a lovely time." Janie took another drink of liquid courage. "In fact, there's something I wanted to talk to you about."

CHAPTER 12

ZADE GLARED AT the pink and orange horizon and jingled the loose change in his pocket. Pesos were a pain in the ass. Every time he went home, he always forgot to exchange them and ended up with a handful that never made a return trip. He had twice as many this time, thanks to shopping with Janie.

Six forty-five. Every time he checked his watch, the thing seemed a little heavier. A weight to remind him of how much he had at stake. He let out a frustrated breath and spun for the seating area by the front desk. She could still show. Janie was smart. Brave. Surely, she'd see the truth in those pictures. She wanted this as much as he did. He knew it the same way he knew what shots to capture.

Arlo poked his head out of the office. "You want a coffee?"

"Nah, man. I'm good."

The bullshit line garnered him a lifted eyebrow from his uncle, but Arlo kept his mouth shut and ducked back to work.

He should've done more to change Janie's mind. Stayed with her and held her while she worked through things. He damn sure shouldn't have left her alone with that nasty stranger's disdain rattling around in her head. God, some people were idiots. Shortsighted, arrogant idiots. Maybe he should go down and check on her. Make sure she was okay.

"I'm the one they're going to judge."

The truth she'd blasted him with cut through him for about the seven-hundredth time. Painful as it was to admit, she was right. No one was going to see him with Janie and waggle a scolding finger his direction. They'd lob it all at her. He could stand beside her, insinuate himself in her defense where he could, but she'd bear the brunt of it every single time.

He pulled the extra thumb drive he'd created last night out of his pocket and plunked down on one of the sofas. What if this was all he had left of her? Hell, he wasn't sure he could even look at the damn photos again if he couldn't follow it up with flesh and blood contact.

A car's engine rumbled behind him, tires squeaking on the cobblestone circular drive. His taxi. Seven o'clock on the dot.

No Janie.

Arlo moseyed out with his hands in his pockets, mouth pursed to one side. "I can ring her room, if you want."

Instinctively, he rubbed the space above his heart, seeking guidance. His dad had been the one to teach him the trick. Shown it to him only months before he died. He'd tapped Zade's sternum and laid his palm over it. *"Right here, son. This is what's important. Listen here."*

He'd listened, but it hadn't worked. She'd asked for space and deserved having her request honored. "Nah." He picked up his carryon and camera bag, and slung them over one shoulder. Holding out both arms, he hugged his uncle. "Thanks for the sweet digs. It made for a helluva visit."

Arlo glared up at him when Zade stepped away, that bushy

dull brown mustache of his hiding the stern line of his mouth. "If she doesn't realize what a good man you are, she doesn't deserve you."

Zade tried for a laugh, but even he wasn't convinced. "Cut her some slack. You didn't see that woman's face. Not fair to judge her for being honest about what she's willing to put up with. People are assholes."

He clapped Arlo on the shoulder. "Tell Aunt Dahlia I said bye."

The only answer he got was a terse nod and a scowl that said Janie's checkout experience wouldn't be as friendly as the check-in.

Five after seven. No one in the lobby except Arlo.

He turned for the green and white taxi idling by the bell stand. Son of a bitch, this hurt.

CHAPTER 13

A KNOCK SOUNDED on the door. "Housekeeping."

Janie jolted upright in bed, heart slogging from a dead standstill to a full-out run. The blackout drapes were pulled tight and tiny streams of sunshine blasted around the edges. The down comforter lay draped across her legs and her phone sat in the middle of the otherwise unmade bed.

What the heck? She'd talked to Mckenna for almost an hour, telling her all about Zade and then—

Oh, damn. So much for just closing her eyes a second.

On the nightstand, an empty glass of wine and an almost empty bottle sat next to the alarm clock. 9:15 AM.

Shit.

She scrambled from the bed. God, she hadn't even changed out of yesterday's swimsuit and cover up. She shoved her flip-flops on, grabbed her bag with one hand and tried to smooth her hair down with the other. It didn't matter. No one around here gave a damn what anyone else looked like anyway. Zade was what was important.

She threw the door open, and the sweet girl who'd tapped at her door jumped back. "*Hola.*"

"Sorry." Janie waved her into the room. "Go ahead." She hurried down the hall, legs pumping as fast as she could without actually running. Oh, to hell with it. She jogged into the nearly empty lobby. For once, a bellman was on duty, a gangly Mexican boy who couldn't be more than eighteen, leaning on the bell stand with his chin propped on his hand looking bored. No Arlo. No guests.

No Zade.

She hustled to the office and paused at the open door. The outer room was empty. IKEA styled cubbies and file cabinets lined the two widest walls and an oblong woven mat in cerulean blue and sunshine yellow stretch over the adobe tiles in the center. Another door stood open in one corner, leading to a well-lit room beyond. From here, all she could see were more cabinets, but the subtle clicks of a keyboard filtered from somewhere inside.

"Arlo?" She knocked on the door jamb.

The clicking stopped.

"Arlo, it's Janie. Can I come in?"

Wheels whirred and clunked against the tiles and someone shuffled in her direction. Arlo strode in, his haphazard appearance the same as always, but the flat mien of his pale blue eyes made her take a step back. "Is there something I can help you with, Ms. McAlister?"

She clutched the door jamb and cleared her throat. "I was supposed to meet Zade this morning. Have you seen him?"

"Oh, I've seen him."

He knew. Damn it all to hell, he knew she was supposed to meet him. "Is he gone?"

"Well, when his taxi came at seven this morning, there certainly wasn't anyone here to stop him, so yes. He's gone."

Her stomach roiled and a sharp, stabbing sensation punched the back of her throat. He thought she didn't want to try. That she didn't want him. "Did he say anything?

124

Leave anything?"

"Why would he?" he snapped.

"I thought he might leave a number. A way to contact him?"

He let out a long, bullish exhalation and glared at her. "The way I understand it, if you didn't show, he leaves you alone. He might be young, Ms. McAlister, but even young men have pride. They shouldn't have to beg. Not for any woman, no matter how special they might be." He turned away and headed into his office.

She lurched forward. "Wait."

Arlo paused and glowered.

She stepped back to the threshold and kept her distance. "I don't blame you for being angry, but I promise you it isn't what it looks like. Can you share his number with me? Let me call him and explain?"

"Why should I? So you can string him along longer and hurt him again the next time some idiot looks cross-eyed at you?"

"It was an accident. I fell asleep. I had every intention of going back to his room, but I drank some wine and I fell asleep."

"You fell asleep?"

"I know," she said. "It sounds terrible, but I hadn't slept much the night before and wine always goes to my head. I didn't mean to—"

"You should have seen him." A flush spread across Arlo's cheeks and his wiry frame shook as he spoke. "He was in here every morning. That boy seldom got up before ten o'clock when he came to visit because he made a point of relaxing and enjoying his time away from work. But you. You had him up bright and early figuring out where he was going to take you next."

She hung her head and tried to swallow around the growing knot in her throat.

"So, no," Arlo said. "I don't think I'll give you his number.

If you want it enough, you'll find a way to get it. Might be good for you to do a little of the chasing for once. See how it feels to put your heart out there, not knowing if the person you're out to impress is going to stomp all over your feelings."

The space behind her breastbone seized and her eyes welled up with tears. Two fat drops fell to the tile at her feet.

"Zade's always positive," he said. "Bright. Even when he was pissed about his business, he knew he was going to find a way to get over it. You managed to dim that light."

He spun and stomped away, but paused at the door to his office. "It's ironic. I always thought it would be a hoot to see Zade get shot down because most women flock to him. After seeing him this morning, I wish like hell I could take that thought back."

"I didn't mean to hurt him," she whispered.

"But you did." And then he was gone.

Laughter rang out behind her. The carefree voices and plodding feet of people headed to the dining hall for a leisurely breakfast. In the distance, a splash sounded. Someone kicking off their day with a dip in the pool.

The bridge of her nose stung and goose bumps fanned out along her skin. She'd hurt him. Badly. Taken all his care and given him pain in return. Arlo was right. She'd flip-flopped on Zade too many times to count. Focused only on herself without a thought for how her actions impacted him.

Selfish. So, damned selfish.

She plodded through the center of the resort, past the pool and down the path to the beach. Her temples throbbed from the wine's lingering effect and her shoulders sagged with a weight she couldn't shake. She paused at the beach's edge.

A couple strolled hand in hand where the water lapped the sand, their feet kicking up tiny drops of water with each step. Naked. Not a stitch of clothes on them.

Janie smiled as much as her heart would allow and waved.

Just like that. Not so much as a flinch at the sight.

Accepting them exactly as they were. Six days ago she'd have run for the hills, or ducked her head in shame or shock. But not anymore. She'd grown.

The wind whipped her hair as she ambled down the beach. She was a fixer. A problem solver. There had to be a way to right the damage she'd caused. But only if she was serious.

Arlo had been right to call her on her fickle behavior. If she managed to find Zade, if he gave her the time of day once she did, she couldn't ping-pong him around anymore. She'd have to talk to him. Stick by him and let him help her out when she hit a rough spot, and vise versa.

God, for a woman who'd been married twenty-two years, she hadn't exactly brought a whole lot of wisdom to the table the second time around. She pottered down the long pier that sheltered the private cove. Her sandals thunked against the wooden slats and the ocean swished all around her, beautiful, sparkling, Caribbean blue.

At the end of the pier, the decking flared out to form a widened observation point. Two lounge chairs sat in one corner, a bright, multi-colored patio umbrella between them and angled to block the harsh afternoon sun. She quickened her steps, eager for the quiet and some time to figure out what to do next.

She rounded the corner and froze.

A woman with gray hair down to her hips and a ruby red sundress lay stretched out in one of the two loungers, propped up to enjoy the view. Her gold bangles winked in the sunshine and her toes were painted happy turquoise. A picture perfect gypsy.

"Oh," Janie said. "I didn't realize anyone was out here."

The woman gazed at the ocean. She smiled, serene and unruffled. Tucked behind one ear was a flower that matched her dress and reminded Janie of an iris, but more tropical. Her voice was a little frail, barely enough to carry over the whistling wind. "Have a seat. Plenty of ocean to go around."

"You sure?"

The smile grew, but her eyes stayed locked in place. She sat forward and patted the cushion of the lounger beside her. "I can't see you, but I can feel your sadness from her. Sit down and let the ocean give you what you need."

She was blind. Surely she wasn't out here alone. One misstep and she'd be neck deep in water, or worse.

The gypsy tapped the cushions again and reclined back in her chair. In her lap was a plain white envelope.

Janie settled in, awkwardness displacing a little of the angst she'd been lugging around since her run-in with Arlo.

"What do you think of Gypsy Cove?" the woman said.

Quirky and definitely unexpected. Though that probably wasn't the kind of answer the woman was after. "It was just what I needed." Janie tugged her cover up further over her thighs. "Have you been here long?"

"Long enough." She inhaled deep and let it out on a slow, measured exhalation. "Would you like to talk about it?"

Funny. Zade would've said the same thing. If she'd taken him up on it, she'd be in a much different headspace right now. "It's a long story."

The woman giggled, a light burden-free sound that spoke of fairies and wind chimes. "Those are the best kind."

Janie smoothed her fingers along the plastic armrest. "Not this one. I mean, I guess it could be, if I can figure out how to fix it."

"Indulge me."

The memory of Zade's pained blue eyes when she'd seen him last flashed bolder than the sun. "I hurt someone. Someone who'd spent a lot of time and effort to help me. Someone who wanted to spend more time with me."

"Mmmm." She folded her arms across her stomach, resting so the envelope couldn't escape the wind's constant push and pull. "And you want to fix it?"

Janie nodded. "I'd like to."

"Then why so sad?"

It felt weird. Sitting here, chatting with a complete stranger about her shortcomings, but liberating at the same time. "Because I don't know if it's fixable. After the way I treated him, he may not want anything to do with me."

The woman kept her silence.

Janie chanced a peek at her and found she'd closed her eyes. So peaceful.

"You're heading home soon?" the gypsy asked, eyes still shut.

"Tomorrow."

"I recommend you give your flight schedule to the man at the desk. He'll be sure to have a car ready for you when it's time to leave."

Janie huffed out an ironic laugh. "I don't think he's going to be too helpful where I'm concerned."

"Arlo? Why on earth wouldn't he?"

"Because the someone I hurt is someone he loves." Janie laid her head back and closed her eyes to match the woman beside her. "I can't say I blame him. I was a bit self-centered."

The woman harrumphed.

Slowly, the throbbing in Janie's head leveled out and her muscles started to uncoil. Zade Painel wasn't a common name, and she knew the general area where he lived. Surely she could track him down. After the conversation she'd had with Mckenna the night before, her daughter would probably have a heyday helping.

Actually, she had a laptop in her room. She could research today. Her flight got in early enough tomorrow that if she found something she might even have time to call Zade when she got home. Or visit.

No, wait. A surprise visit wasn't the best idea. Kind of stalkerish, really.

For the first time since she'd woken to the knock on her door, her heart upped its pace for something besides panic. She could do this. If Zade wasn't willing to give things a go, she'd face it when the time came. The good Lord knew she'd earned a solid setback, but doing nothing wasn't an option.

The lady beside her chuckled. "I can almost hear your brain from here. Has the universe given you your plan so quickly?"

The universe? Someone else had used "the universe" this week, but for the life of her she couldn't remember who.

"Did you find what you came for, Ms. McAlister?"

Janie perked up. "How do you know my name?"

The gypsy opened her eyes and grinned. Her gaze might not connect to any of the beauty that surrounded her, but it twinkled to match the water on the waves. "You first. Did you find what you came for?"

No. Not exactly. She'd thought she'd figure out what to tactically do with her life. Maybe plot out downsizing from her big house and target some charities to fill her growing chunk of available time. Instead, she'd found something more. Something so much better. Bigger. "I found myself."

"I'm glad. I find it's so much easier to hold my head up and champion what I know is right when I'm solid in my own beliefs and what I want for my life." She smoothed the letter in her lap and ducked her head for a minute, thoughtful. "You live near Dallas, am I right?"

Tingles scampered across Janie's shoulders and down her spine. Her mouth ran dry and she fisted her hands in her lap. "I do."

The woman handed the envelope to Janie. "Getting to the post office is such a chore for me these days and I hate to give my Arlo extra things to do. Would you be a dear and drop this in the mail for me when you get home? I didn't get much time to sit and visit with my nephew this trip. Word has it he was busy with a lady friend he made while he was here."

Zade Painell
2411 N Hall Street #27
Dallas TX 75204

* * *

"You're Dahlia."

Dahlia laid her head back and closed her eyes. "I am."

"You know what happened?"

"I do."

"And you trust me?"

She rolled her head toward Janie and opened her sightless eyes. Blue. The same color as Zade's. "You're willing to own your mistakes and face the consequences, and Zade's a smart man with excellent judgment. He trusts you, so I trust you."

She faced forward and stared out at the sea. "Now, go. Claim what it is you want and make my boy happy."

CHAPTER 14

"*LADIES AND GENTLEMEN, on behalf of your flight crew, we'd like to be the first to welcome you to Dallas/Ft. Worth. The time here is two fifteen and the temperature is a scorching one hundred and two. We'd ask that you please lower your blinds to help us keep the cabin temperature down while we disembark.*"

Janie pulled the window cover beside her shut and stifled a groan of frustration. Damn, but her nails were a mess. Then again, an antsy woman stuck three hours in an international airport and two and half hours on a flight would ruin even the best manicure.

"*As we approach the gate, we'd like to remind you to remain in your seat with your seatbelt fastened until the captain has turned off the fasten seatbelt sign overhead. We know you have a choice when you travel and we appreciate you choosing our airline.*"

Two fifteen. Another thirty to get her bags from baggage claim. Mckenna and Thomas were due to pick her up at three. Plenty of time to put the plan she'd worked with her kids into play before nightfall.

The big, burly man in the center seat grunted as he leaned forward and pulled his laptop back out from under the space in front of him. "You got big plans or you just hate flying?"

Janie checked her seat back pocket for the thirtieth time. No trash. Phone in her purse. "Hmmm?"

The man beside her chuckled. "I asked what's got you so jumpy."

"Me?"

"Yup."

She flipped through her purse. The letter was right where she'd left it. "What makes you think I'm jumpy?"

"Because that knee of yours hasn't quit jiggling since take off."

She planted her foot flat on the floor. "Sorry."

He laughed good naturally and flicked his seatbelt open way before the sign turned off.

Ding.

Thank God. Janie surged upright as far as the overhead bin would let her, and organized her stuff. Normally the chaos of traveling didn't bother her, but right now all she could think about was taking charge and getting the twelve rows in front of her out of her way.

She hit the jet way with long strides, her thighs eking out a none-to-subtle reminder that she'd spent the last seven days mostly on her ass. She bet she'd put on ten pounds.

Well, maybe not. What she'd gained days one through five might have been offset by her limited intake for the last two. She sure as heck hadn't touched any more wine.

Huddled with the rest of her fellow travelers, she glared at the electronic sign above her baggage carousel as if that might somehow hurry their bags' appearance. A phone call to Zade was the safe bet. She'd thought she wouldn't have a choice but to use Dahlia's letter and reach out to him face to face, but then Mckenna had jumped on the bandwagon and tracked down his phone number in a whopping thirty minutes.

No, calling was the easy way. He'd taken chance after chance for her. This was a time for her to be brave. To do exactly what Arlo suggested. Chase after Zade and lay her heart out there. To let him know she was serious.

The long, grating buzzer sounded and the travelers jostled for position around the bin. The bags rode into view at a glacial pace. It figured, hers would be one of the last.

Two fifty. Ten more minutes. She'd ride home with her kids, drop off her suitcases, and freshen up a bit. Maybe she'd wear one of the sundresses Zade had talked her into buying downtown. The deep emerald green accented her newly acquired tan and made her hair stand out. God knew, he liked her hair.

Yep. The sundress would be perfect. She slowed her steps to match the painfully slow automatic rotating doors and punched out into the gruesome Texas heat. Ugh. Definitely freshening up first. Hard to wow a guy and talk him into a second chance with wilted hair and blotched makeup.

She pulled her phone out of her purse and thumbed to her text messages. *Waiting at Terminal E,* she typed to Mckenna. Thomas would be driving and she didn't dare text him. No matter how many times she told him it was bad to text and drive, he refused to listen. Typical Thomas. Always thinking he knew better.

Pulling in now, her daughter typed back. Amazing, how fast her kids could operate technology. But she'd get there too. Her life was about to take a seriously different turn, one way or another.

Sure enough, her silver Lexus RX came around the corner and angled for the inside lane. Her kids hopped out and the hatch opened on a slow glide.

"Mckenna." She hugged her baby girl and let out a relieved breath. She was here, her kids were on board with her plans, and everything would work out. She hoped.

"Wow, you weren't kidding," Thomas said to Mckenna as he reached for his hug.

Janie held him as long as he'd let her with so many people puttering around. "Right about what?"

"That you were hyped up like a whacked out One Direction freak." Thomas let her go and stepped back. "Not sure why you're in such a hurry, though. You've got his address and I doubt he's gonna disappear overnight. Need to play it cool. Not rush it."

"Oh, shut up, Tommy," Mckenna said and turned to Janie. "He won't admit it, but he's the one that jumped in and found Zade's phone number."

Janie grinned at her son and motioned to the bags. "Okay, lets get loaded up. Got lots to do."

Thomas laughed and reached for her bag.

"I'll get that." The voice came up from behind her, breathless and bright.

Before she could turn, someone reached for her bag and lifted it. Strong hands, long fingers, delicious tan.

Zade.

He picked her bag up and cupped her nape. "Can't believe I almost missed you."

"You're here." Had she said it out loud or merely thought it? His touch and warmth battered the apprehension she'd held since yesterday. Here. With her. She couldn't get past any more than that, his touch scrambling her thoughts and motor skills.

"Arlo called me." His thumb back and forthed against her neck, slow and comforting. "Told me when you'd be in."

The flight schedule. She'd given the information to a very begrudging Arlo as Dahlia had suggested. Sneaky, sneaky woman.

"That okay?" he said.

"More than okay." Her heart made up for the beats it had missed since she'd heard his voice, and she felt light enough to float away if the Texas heat allowed the slightest breeze. "I was coming home to find you."

"Yeah, he told me that too." He leaned in and pressed a

soft, lingering kiss on her lips. "I couldn't wait that long."

Thomas cleared his throat.

"Oh." Janie pulled away and smoothed her hand across her stomach. It didn't help. The flutters wouldn't stop. "Zade, these are my kids. Thomas and Mckenna."

Zade offered his hand to Thomas first, then Mckenna. "Good to meet you."

Good grief. Her fuddled mind finally kicked into gear as Zade hefted her bags and loaded them into the back of the SUV. "You're all dressed up."

Pale blue shirt, tan business slacks, and navy blue sport coat. Not exactly a boardroom three piece suit, but still sexy as hell in a cover model kind of way. His hair looked different too. The same length, but more polished in the way it was styled.

"Met with my attorney this morning. That's why I almost missed you." He reached for the overnight bag she'd slung on her shoulder. "I signed the paperwork to get my business back."

She clenched her purse strap tighter and fought the urge to bounce up and down like a giddy seven-year old. She'd really helped him.

Mckenna sidled up beside her and muttered, "I thought you said he was young. He looks old enough to me."

Zade closed the hatch and met her gaze, an eyebrow lifted.

Her chest tightened and her vision blurred with a trace of tears. He'd come for her. He'd fought for her. And looking at her the way he was right now, she felt nothing short of invincible.

She stepped off the curb and laid her hand above his heart. Its solid, steady rhythm pounded beneath her palm, as powerful and stalwart as the man it beat for. Wherever they went from here was up to them. Two free-spirited souls making their way despite convention. "It doesn't matter how old he is. He's what I want."

EPILOGUE

ZADE ZIGZAGGED THROUGH the still unopened moving boxes scattered through the living room and shouted up the hardwood staircase. "Janie, babe, hurry up. We're going to be late."

"Almost done!" As muted as her voice sounded, Janie had to be deep in the master bedroom closet. Probably still grumbling over his last minute announcement they had a business meeting. "What kind of clients are they, anyway? And where did you say we were meeting them?"

"I didn't say." And he wouldn't either. Too much information and she'd clue in to his plans sooner than he wanted. "And it's just a consult on engagement shots. No big deal. Just throw something on and let's go."

Quick footsteps sounded above him, rounding through the bedroom and out onto the landing. She tossed a set of sandals to the ground, and peered over the wrought iron cat walk that overlooked the main living area. Her loose white cotton skirt and matching tank gave her a just-off-the-beach look, and a bold red belt accented her waist. Shoving a set of bracelets on her wrist, she checked the Old English clock mounted over the stonework fireplace. Her wild auburn hair hung loose and wavy on either side of her head. "I still can't believe I overlooked an appointment. I never do that."

"You didn't overlook anything. I booked it."

"Since when do you book appointments anymore?" She slipped into her shoes and headed for the stairs.

"Since you were busy cramming for finals and coordinating our move." He'd hoped planning his surprise in the middle of all the chaos might throw Janie off the scent, but seeing how panicked the curveball made her, he kind of wished he'd taken a different route.

He held up her briefcase and purse as she reached the landing. "You know, once upon a time, I booked all my own appointments."

"That's before we made your studio Dallas' go-to photography place." Slinging her too-heavy bag onto one shoulder, she grinned and leaned in for a peck on his cheek. "Now, you've got me."

And Mckenna, and Thomas, and three interns. In the two years since they'd come back from Gypsy Cove, Janie's kids had zeroed in on their own business dreams—Mckenna declaring her major in graphic design, and Thomas signing up with a big name marketing firm in downtown Dallas. When they weren't driving toward their own goals, they put their time and attention into Gypsy Studios. "I wouldn't have it any other way."

He steered her to the front door, but Janie dug in her heels. "Wait. The car's in the garage, remember? You pulled it around after the movers left."

"Yeah, I know. We're meeting them across the street." That was the nice thing about their new house. Two blocks in either direction and they had their pick of some of lower Greenville's best restaurants and bars. "I've got a reservation at Blue Goose."

"We're meeting a client at a Mexican restaurant?"

"Well, yeah. It's Saturday. Who wants a stuffy office meeting on a Saturday afternoon?" He opened the door and ushered her out, locking the door behind them. "Trust me. It'll be fine."

From the sidewalk, Janie stared back at their new home. Or, more accurately put, renovated home. For the last six months they'd used all their spare time together refurbishing the prairie-style home. Even before they'd finished the place, they'd spent many a late winter and spring night on the wide, wrap-around porch, Janie's whimsical landscaping all around them. "We did good. We did real good."

"Yeah, we did." He kissed her forehead and pulled her tight to his side. "Now let's get this done and get home so we can tackle a few more boxes. I swear those movers misplaced half my stuff."

Five minutes later, they wound their way through the restaurant's growing afternoon crowd toward the wait stand. As atmosphere went, the Blue Goose was seriously old school. Plain concrete floors stretched wall to wall, and gaudy sky-blue and flamingo pink paint covered every paintable surface. The food and drinks, however, couldn't be beat. Plus, the place was loud enough to ensure Janie wouldn't have clue what she was in for until it was too late.

The hostess caught sight of he and Janie wandering her direction and perked up, a picture worthy smile on her face. "Mr. Painel! We're all ready for you."

Janie glanced back. "How'd you get a reservation? They never make reservations here."

And this was why he'd had to be careful. Thank God, they were ten steps away from most of the charade being over. Nothing ever got past Janie. With a hand at her back, he urged her to follow the hostess. "Yeah, well, sometimes you get lucky."

Before she could argue, they rounded the thick wall that separated the bar from the open table seating.

"Surprise!"

Janie staggered back a step, and Zade steadied her with a hand at her shoulder.

All of Janie's friends and family stood with margaritas raised and big smiles on their faces. Centered in the middle were Mckenna and Thomas, their phones aimed and catching every candid moment. Balloons in every color were anchored at each table, and a huge *Happy Graduation* banner was strung across the middle of the room.

Glancing back over one shoulder, Janie smirked. "I knew I didn't miss an appointment."

"No, babe. You never miss anything."

For the next two hours, he couldn't get a minute of her to himself. Presents were given, stories told, and copious numbers of margaritas were consumed. Janie beamed, flittering between her guests in the comfortably canny way she always did, making everyone feel at home even when they weren't.

"Okay, the deed is done." Mckenna sidled up beside him, a devious grin on her face and her cheeks flushed. She held out the spare key to his house and winked. "Mission Homerun is on schedule."

Thomas came up behind her and clamped a hand on her shoulder. "You've had entirely too much fun with all this."

"Yeah, and it's been worth it." Her focus locked onto Janie saying goodbye to the last of her guests. "Did you see the look on her face?"

"Okay, I'll grant you that one." Thomas grinned at Zade. "I'll bet you get an even better shocker in before the night's done."

Zade fisted his hand around the folded, worn note in his pants pocket. The nerves he'd been wrestling with all day surged to full throttle and made him damn glad he'd bypassed his usual enchilada special. "We'll see. I'm not putting pressure on her."

Thomas shook his head. "You don't give yourself enough

140

credit. She's more alive since she met you. Happier and confident. She's not going to let the man who gave her that go."

"Hey, you two ready?" Janie's ex, Gerald, shuffled from the entrance.

Janie's voice cut in before Mckenna or Thomas could answer, her easy strides bringing her into the group. "Gerald, why didn't you come to the party?"

Gerald's eyes darted between Zade and Janie. "Zade offered, but I didn't want you to be uncomfortable." At forty-five, he was a pretty fit guy, only his slightly thinning black hair giving any indication he was stomping through midlife. In the two years Zade had been with Janie, he'd used his looks to snag a string of younger women, none of which seemed to stick.

As if remembering where he was, Gerald shook his head and held out a small, wrapped package. "I hope it's okay. I got you a little something. Nothing big."

Janie tore into the gift wrap. "You didn't have to get me anything." Still, her eyes glinted with curiosity and her lips were parted in surprise. She opened the box and beamed. "My own charm." She turned it around so Zade could see. "It's just like the one I got Mckenna when she graduated."

Nestled in navy blue felt, was one of those high-end charms Mckenna was always angling for, this one in the form of a graduation cap with a tassel hanging off to one side.

Janie wrapped Gerald up in fond hug. "Thanks, Gerald. It was sweet of you to get it for me."

It should have been awkward, if not for everyone else, then at least for Zade, but somehow it wasn't. Somewhere along the way, their friends and family had accepted his and Janie's relationship, Gerald included. A fact he was hoping would work in his favor before the night was through.

"So." Gerald stepped away and eyeballed his kids. "You two ready?"

"What?" Janie's gaze shifted between Mckenna and

Thomas. "You're not staying? I thought you two would stay at our house?"

"Not tonight." Mckenna winked at Zade, a move Janie would surely lock onto. "Dad's got a thing he wants us to go to, but we'll come over tomorrow. That sound good?"

Sure enough, Janie's gaze whipped to Zade and she cocked her head to one side. "What's that all about?"

Zade raised his hands and tried to blank his expression, no easy task with the weight of everyone's stares aimed solely on him. "Don't look at me. I'm all out of graduation surprises." Not a complete lie. Not with the graduation disclaimer tacked on for good measure. "I am ready to find the rest of my stuff, though. Two of my cameras are missing and I need one of them before my shoot on Monday. Unless you need more graduation excitement?"

Janie pursed her mouth and narrowed her eyes.

Mckenna kissed her mom on the cheek, pulling Janie out of her considering stare. "See you tomorrow, mom. Don't stay up too long unpacking. I need to go shopping tomorrow."

The intercession did the trick, pulling Janie into lingering goodbyes with her kids while they ambled out to the street. It wasn't until they were back at their house and ambling through the front door that Janie circled back around with her suspicions. "What was the wink for?"

Zade kicked off his loafers near the front door and tossed his keys to the end table, keeping his eyes anywhere but on Janie. "The wink?"

"Yeah, the wink."

Five minutes. Five minutes and a few well placed words to get her where he wanted her, and he could let down his guard. He steeled himself and turned, wrapping her up and pulling her close. "You're imagining things, babe. Mckenna was just still wound up from coordinating the party. He palmed the back of her head, her soft curls bunching in his palm in a way that never got old. "Tell you what, how about we just target a few boxes tonight. If we don't find my cameras in the next twenty minutes or so, we'll ditch the search and start over tomorrow." He dipped in close and slid his nose alongside hers, teasing her lips. "I'll give you my own special graduation present in bed."

Her lips curled against his and she nipped his lower lip. "Now that sounds like a present I'd like."

Thank God. Re-direction accomplished. "Good. You go change and see if there are any promising boxes to start with upstairs. I'll get the box knife."

"Okay." She pulled away, grinned in a way that promised all kinds of mischief, and sashayed up the stairs.

So close. Another few minutes and he'd learn if things would fall together the way he hoped. The way he wanted more than anything.

He pulled the letter from his pocket and unfolded it. Janie had delivered his Aunt Dahlia's letter the same day she'd come back from Gypsy Cover and he'd read it every day since. Some days more than once. The paper was soft and crumpled, parts of the pencil message smudged. Not that it mattered. Zade knew it almost by heart.

Words can't express how proud I am of you. How you've become your own man, and yet still echo your father's passion. He'd be proud of you, too. Particularly in the woman you've chosen.

I know it's not yet time, but when your heart speaks...when it urges you to jump...take the leap. Ignore the naysayers and critics, and treasure your gift. Your love. Lift your woman up and let her soar, and know that she will do the same for you. Only promise me that you'll visit your dear Aunt Dahlia so that I can hear the happiness in your voice and feel your smiles all around me.

Janie's voice floated down from the master bedroom. "Where did this box come from?"

Showtime. "What box?"

"There's one in our bedroom. It wasn't here when we left."

No, there hadn't been. This one Mckenna had delivered

mid-party. He grabbed the box knife he'd left on the fireplace mantel. "You probably just missed it since we were in a hurry. What's it labeled?"

"Studio. But I didn't miss it."

Zade jogged up the stairs, his heart pounding so hard it was a wonder it didn't just give up altogether.

Janie stood in the middle of the room, her hands on both hips, and a suspicious pucker on her lips. The box was a big one, nearly reaching her hips. "What gives?"

Zade shrugged and moseyed to the box. He tried to keep the smile off his face, but it didn't work. "Beats me." He offered the knife. "Probably the one I'm looking for."

Her lips twitched, but she took the knife and sliced the packing tape open. Prying the flaps aside, she tossed fistful after fistful of packing paper to either side of the box. She was nearly to the bottom, her body almost folded in half and her hips deliciously displayed over the edge. "There's nothing in here."

"You sure?"

She tossed out one more wad of paper and froze. Slowly, she stood, a tiny box with a gold base and a black top pinched between her fingers. Her cheeks were a pretty pink and her eyes were huge. Her voice rasped against his strained nerves, all husky and deep. "I don't think this is a camera."

His own voice came out a little jagged and broken. "I don't think it is either."

"Zade…"

"Open it."

She swallowed, her eyes locked on him for long seconds before she pulled the lid free and let her gaze slide to what sat inside. "Oh, Zade…"

He circled behind her and pulled her back against his chest, his arms banded around her waist. The engagement ring winked up from its black velvet pillow, three ropes intertwined with pavé diamonds and a two carat solitaire in the center. "Do you like it?"

"It's huge."

"Babe, you manage our books. I can't imagine you've missed you've tripled our bottom line in one year. We can afford it."

Her fingers tightened on the box before she laid one of her hands over his at her waist. Resting her head on his chest, she looked up at him. "I love how you call the studio ours."

As if he could call it anything else. Since the day he'd met her, imagining anything without Janie in the equation had been impossible. "Our clothes are in the same closet. Our names are on the same mortgage. We work in the same office. The only thing that's missing is my ring on your finger. I want to make everything an 'ours.'"

Looking back at the ring, she traced the center diamond with one trembling finger.

She couldn't say no. Well, she could, but he wasn't sure how he'd handle it if she did. He hadn't allowed his thoughts to go there. Hadn't planned for how to tackle anything but yes. "You don't have to decide tonight. Just sit with it a while."

"I don't have to wait."

Fear and hope wrestled in his stomach and the knot in his throat grew bigger than his fist.

Janie turned in his arms, her eyes wet with tears and her smile brighter than a full moon. She rubbed her palm over his sternum the same way he always did when he wasn't sure what to do. "I know what I want. More now than I ever have before in my life. I want to be your wife. I want to focus on our business and watch it grow. I want you with me as I watch my kids build their own lives." She raised up on her tip toes and pressed a soft kiss to his lips. "And I want to adopt a little boy."

She said yes. That she wanted to be his wife. Over and over again her words shot through his head. Building their lives, their business, having a kid—

His thoughts screeched to a halt. "I told you, babe. I'm in this for you, whatever that looks like. We don't need a kid to make us whole."

"No, we don't. But I see you with my kids, how you've left your mark on their lives. In two years you've become their friend and their mentor. Robbing this world of your influence on a young mind would be a waste. I want that for you, and for us. I want to see it in action."

A kid. Someone he could spend time with the way his dad did with him. As bold as if they'd happened yesterday, flashes of time he'd spent with his day burned bright in his mind. Fishing with his dad. Holding his hand while they ran errands for his mom on Saturday. Helping him change the oil on his beat up GTO.

"You should see your face right now," Janie said. "I know you say you don't need it, but you'd be a great dad. And there are so many kids out there to love." She curled her arms around his neck and swayed, her head tilted in a carefree, sexy pose worthy of a twenty by thirty canvas. "Say yes."

God, she was amazing. Sweet and open, opening herself up to a life he hadn't even dared to imagine. "I thought 'say yes' was my line."

"It was, and I jumped all over your offer. I think you should return the favor, and give me what I want."

His fingers tightened on the back of her neck and her warm breath fluttered against his face. Who would have thought a bad business deal would have brought him such a perfect life? Fate was, indeed, a mysterious and powerful creature, not unlike his soon-to-be wife.

"I love you, Janie." He kissed her full lips and drew in her sweet scent. "For as long as I live, I'll always give you what you want."

Be sure to check out Book One in The Eden Series

From Rhenna Morgan

Unexpected Eden

Now available from Kensington's Lyrical Press

Chapter 1

Slow breaths in, slow breaths out. All Lexi had to do was focus on the thump of Rihanna's latest hit, keep the drinks flowing, and stick to her half of the bar. The mother lode of testosterone on Jerry's side couldn't sit there all night. Could he?

"Don't suppose you've noticed, but there's a scrumptious not-from-around-here type giving you the eyeball." Mindy grinned and handed over the latest round of drink orders.

White t-shirt, killer muscles, and dark chocolate hair halfway down his back? Yeah, she'd noticed. Repeatedly. And every time she went for a visual refill, his silver gaze shocked nerve endings she'd long thought dead.

"Drop it, Mindy. Guys like that are an occupational hazard and you know it."

"Honey, that man is way past hazard. More like Chernobyl." She leaned into the trendy concrete countertop. The modern pendant lights spotlighted her platinum hair and ample cleavage. One thing about Mindy—she knew how to work her assets. "I'll bet the fallout's worth it."

"It's packed tonight. You gonna get those drinks out and stash a few tips, or waste 'em on eye candy?"

Mindy's dreamy smile melted and she pulled the loaded cocktail tray close. "All work and no play, huh?" She shook her head and turned for the crowd. "Have fun with that."

Well, hell. Another social interaction down the toilet. At twenty-five-years-old, you'd think she could handle a little female bonding in the form of man-ogling. Especially when four of those years had been spent tending bar. But damn it, some things weren't meant for discussion. Her overactive man-jitters being one of them.

Crouching to snag a fresh bottle of vodka beneath the counter, she peeked behind her.

Lips guaranteed to make a girl forget her name curled into a sly smile.

Busted.

She spun away too fast and scraped her forehead against the rough edge of the bar. "Son of a fucking, no good piece of shit." Head down, she counted to three and fought the need to check for witnesses, thankful the music was loud enough to cover her curse. The graceless gawker routine wasn't normally her deal, but for the last thirty minutes she'd come up woefully short in the finesse department—and it was all the dark-haired man's fault.

New bottle ready for action, she faced two middle-aged men dressed like frat boys and settled into her pour-and-bill groove. The routine was a comfort, a stabilizing rhythm to counterbalance the ever-present gaze heavy on her back.

"Hey, Lex." Jerry smacked her shoulder and motioned behind him, never breaking stride as he headed for the register. "Tall, dark and handsome wants to see you."

She wouldn't look. Not again. The giggling trio of barely legal blondes fighting their way into ordering range wasn't nearly as nice on the eyes, but at least they kept her anchored. "Since when did you take up matchmaking?"

"Since the guy offered me a Benjamin to make sure it was you who took care of him."

What? She spun.

The stranger met her surprised stare head on, his smirk a potent mix of humble and confident. "Sold me down the river, did you?"

"Damn right." Jerry winked, shoved a stack of wrinkled bills into the register, and swaggered toward the waiting blondes without so much as a wish for good luck.

Lexi huffed and took an order from the none-too-shabby twenty-something guy right in front of her on principle. Mystery man could cool his jets for a minute or two. Besides, if his banter matched his looks, she'd need every second she could get to batten down the hatches.

She filled orders with slow deliberation and an extra bit of bravado, grabbing snippets of recon where she could.

A vicious looking man sat next to her dark-haired hunk. Lazy raven waves fell to a hard jawline, a tightly trimmed goatee making his harsh face a downright menace. Entirely the wrong selection for wingman material.

Out of customers and bar space, she faced both men and wiped down of the counter. "What can I get you?" The catchall phrase came out shakier than she wanted, and tried to cover it with an intensive, yet completely unnecessary study of the bottles stocked below the counter.

"You disliked my tactic." God help her, the man had a voice to match his face. An easy glide that left a slow burn in its wake. Kind of like fifty-year-old Scotch. "I admit it's not my style, but I was desperate."

Not exactly the approach she'd expected from a hottie, but it did help ease her tension. "There's not a thing desperate about you and we both know it."

He answered with a megawatt smile that damn near knocked her off her feet. Utterly relaxed, he rested muscled forearms on the bar and raised an eyebrow. "Have dinner with me."

She shouldn't be able to hear him in such a crush, let alone register a physical impact, but damned if she wasn't processing both loud and clear. "I don't even know you."

He offered his hand. Long, strong fingers stretched out, showing calluses along his palm. "Eryx Shantos."

Wingman stared straight ahead, his aqua eyes cold enough to freeze a soul.

"Lexi Merrill." As their palms met, a rush fired up her arm and down her spine, and she shook as though she'd cozied up to a blow dryer in a bathtub. She ripped her hand away and rubbed the tingling center up and down her jean-clad hip.

Eryx didn't so much as blink, his sword-colored gaze glinting with dare and determination.

Maybe fatigue was taking a toll on her imagination. Or the flu. Or a desperate need to get laid. Gripping the bar for support, she took an order from a cute little brunette trying to avoid a middle-aged, bald guy's come-on.

Except for a slow pull off his beer, Wingman stayed stock-still. His angry expression screamed, "Stay the fuck back."

"Now you know me," Eryx said. "Have dinner with me."

"I have to work."

"Then lunch."

"I work then too." A lame excuse, but true. Two jobs and part-time college didn't leave a lot of room for being social. Not that socializing ever managed to work in her favor.

"Breakfast, then."

A half-hearted laugh slipped out before she could stop it. "You're persistent, I'll give you that."

"You have nooo idea." Wingman tipped his longneck for another drink, fingers loose around the dark glass despite his tight voice.

Eryx shot him a nasty glare.

"Your friend doesn't talk much." Lexi grabbed a few empties and dunked them in a tub of soapy water.

"His name's Ludan. And he may not be able to talk at all by the time the night's over. Depends on if he manages to keep his tongue intact."

"Yo! Need a few Bud Lights." Two college-age men in need of a manners class shoved their way to Ludan's free side.

Ludan straightened and pushed the men back a handful of steps with nothing more than a glare.

No way was she dealing with the fallout from a brawl, even if the young punks could use the lesson. "Stand down and kill the scary badass routine."

Ludan faced her, his eyes a shade closer to white than blue. It took a tense breath or two, but the muscles beneath his black t-shirt relaxed and he smirked. He eased down on his barstool and snagged his beer. "Your woman's got bite, Eryx."

She snatched a pair of Buds from the cooler and popped the tops off. "I'm not his woman."

"Not yet." Eryx's calm retort landed between them—part taunt, part promise. The sheer resoluteness in his expression sent a rush she didn't dare analyze clear to her toes.

Better to get down to business and add some distance before

she did something she'd regret. "Tell me what you want to drink. I gotta get back to work."

"I've already told you want I want."

Lexi planted a hand on her hip and thanked God he couldn't see her pounding heart. "A tall order that's not on the menu."

Eryx nodded, a slow, sultry move that intimated a whole lot more than simple agreement. "Some things are worth waiting for."

A blast of déjà vu hit and left her stunned. A hot gush of frustration shoved in behind it and spun her back toward her half of the bar. With a thump on Jerry's arm, she motioned toward Eryx. "He's all yours. I want the sane side back."

She worked her portion of the crowd with single-minded enthusiasm. Worth waiting for. It was just a line. Guys like Eryx were landmines waiting for a trigger.

A couple nuzzled nose to nose, an out-of-place intimacy amid the harsh lights from the dance floor. Her heart stuttered. Was she bypassing something good? Maybe she should circle back. See if he needed another—

He was gone, his wingman with him. A gaggle of women, one with a naughty tiara and last-night-of-freedom sash wrapped around her, crowded between the leather and chrome barstools.

The tiny thread of hope she'd refused to acknowledge snapped in half. She snatched a bag of ice from the back cooler and shook it over the longnecks along the front bin of the bar. She knew better than to wish for things like love. Hell, she hadn't even done a double take on a guy in more years than she could count. She could get a massage from a team of Chippendales and she probably wouldn't get excited. What made her think she'd ever find anyone worth laying her heart on the line?

She turned for the rear register and shoved her disappointment deep. Better to study that topic later—say in about five years. She'd finish out the night, prep for tomorrow like she always did, and be glad she'd avoided the drama.

Pinpricks raced down her spine and warmth surrounded her. Not the slick and humid dance floor variety, but comforting, infused with leather and sandalwood. Out of place. Delicious.

Ordinary patrons reflected in the wide mirror before her, faces bright with the glaze of alcohol. Nothing stood out. No danger.

But she could have sworn warm, rough fingertips grazed her cheek.

Perched on the high retaining wall at the end of the parking lot, Eryx glared at the streetlight overhead. One flick of his wrist and he could fry the whole damned contraption with an electric pulse. Better on his patience for sure, but not so great for his plans. Smart women like Lexi weren't usually keen on dark parking lots at two-thirty in the morning.

Tapping his boot heels against the wall, Ludan cracked his knuckles and scanned their surroundings for the fiftieth time. As Eryx's somo, Ludan looked out for his wellbeing, but the nasty bastard sometimes took the job too deep into mother hen territory. "We need to go back to Eden. Recharge for a few days and then come make a play for your woman. If the Rebellion catches us here with our energy this low—"

"The rumors are just that. Rumors." Eryx shifted on the cold concrete, anything to get the blood flow back into his too-stationary ass. "The Rebellion hasn't launched an attack worth merit in over seventy years. I bet I couldn't find five people who've seen Maxis in more than that. I'm not cranking my men into a tizzy over hypotheticals."

"And the ellan?" Ludan's cool gaze slid to Eryx. "You gonna keep ignoring them too? The old coots are chomping at the bit to know what's got you so tied up in the human realm."

"Only half of them are old coots. The rest are as young and eager to modernize our race as we are." If you could call one hundred and fifty-two years old young. From the human perspective, it probably seemed closer to eternity.

Ludan looked away and gripped the ledge. Better than throwing a punch—which would probably be his preference.

Hard to blame the guy. Ten years helping Eryx look for the woman who visited his dreams every night would send most people running. Ludan? Loyal to the core and still right here with him. But that didn't mean he'd give up on his argument. Ten more seconds tops before he chimed in again. Ten. Nine. Eight. Se—

"You're the malran. You call the shots." Ludan crossed his arms. "But even without the Rebellion threat, you're risking your throne and a death sentence."

And there it was. The lecture he'd had coming since he finally tracked a clue from his dreams to Lexi's workplace. Humans were a no-no. Do business with them? Walk freely in their realm? Tangle in a bout of good, hot, sweaty sex? All fair game. Fill them in on the Myren race or interfere in human destiny? That shit earned you the axe, a mandate passed down by The Great One himself when he'd created Eryx's people.

"We've been here too long," Ludan said. "Both our powers are damned near gone. Any attack outside of one-to-one and we're screwed."

The service door kachunked open.

Eryx shoved off the ledge.

"Sorry, man." The bartender he'd bribed ambled toward the mid-size pickup on Eryx's left with a sympathetic shake of his head. "You've got it bad."

Eryx leaned against the brick wall, crossed his arms, and notched one boot over his ankle. "You telling me she's not worth the trouble?"

The man's keys jangled against the quiet night and a perky chirp mixed with a flash of headlights. He shrugged and tugged open the driver's door. "Hard to say. Never met a man who made it through the gauntlet." He tossed his black duffel bag across to the passenger's side, shot a man-to-man nod at Ludan then smirked at Eryx. "Good luck."

"Fan-fucking-tastic. Your dream woman's the hard-to-get type." As the truck pulled away, Ludan leapt to the asphalt and planted his hands on his hips. "We're never getting home."

Crickets and the drone of cars on the interstate filled the silence.

"Would you go back if you were me?" It was an underhanded question. Ludan knew the toll Lexi's dream visits took on his ability to reason. How he woke strung out with need, zeroed in on the single purpose of finding his mate. "If you were this close, would you risk losing her?"

Ludan didn't exactly hang his head in defeat, but he sure studied the asphalt hard. "No." He turned and stuffed his hands in his pockets. "Better not to fuck with The Fates."

The door rattled and eased open.

His skin buzzing, Eryx pushed to full height.

Ludan sidled further away and switched to telepathy. "You sure you wanna do this? You can't be sure she's Myren."

"I'll figure it out. The pictures in her mind were definitely of Eden."

Under the unforgiving street lamps, Lexi's tan skin glowed.

Soft-black hair brushed her shoulders and her hips swayed, slow with an unpretentious sexuality. A distracted frown tugged at her lips, her face downcast. She looked up and froze, bits of gravel crunching beneath her fancy shoes. "You gotta be kidding me."

"I told you I was willing to wait." He tried for a lighthearted tone, no easy task. A decade of tracking one irresistible woman did crazy things to a man's insides.

She zigzagged a look between Eryx near her red Jeep Wrangler and Ludan a stone's throw away then glanced at the closed door behind her. She adjusted the purse strap at her shoulder and narrowed her blue-gray eyes. "You're one step past stalker."

He held up his hands. "I swear it's not like that. I really do want to take you to breakfast." So he'd gone a little further with his scan of her memories when they'd shaken hands than he should have. She always caught an after-work breakfast with a man who looked to be in his mid to late fifties, and she drove the Wrangler parked behind him.

"It's nearly three AM."

"And we're all hungry. Perfect timing." He lowered his hands and hoped Ludan wasn't sporting his perma-scowl. Non-threatening wasn't his strong suit.

"Smart girls don't go to breakfast with strangers." She nodded toward her Jeep. "Let alone get near a vehicle with unknown men nearby."

"Your bartender pal clued me in." Hopefully, she'd buy the lie, not that it felt good on his tongue. "And you could always call a friend to join us. Public place, your own car." He paused to let the idea sink in. "What's there to lose?"

A breeze ruffled her loose hair. Her face slackened and a flutter of energy drifted across the parking lot, barely perceptible.

Ludan perked up.

It was Lexi. It had to be. Humans couldn't generate such a ripple—at least not any he'd ever met.

She tugged her purse to her chest and rooted around inside. "Waffle House. A few miles down the road." A wad of keys settled in her palm, she dropped the purse back to her hip. "I meet a friend there after work. A cop, just to be clear. So don't get any ideas."

Satisfaction fired hot in his veins, the fact some strange older man would be along for the ride a paltry detail. He closed the distance, slow and steady, and traced the angle of her cheekbone.

Her eyes widened.

The Fates were never wrong. They might be coy with their reasons and damned vague in their instructions, but there was one thing he was sure of. They'd led him to his mate.

About the Author

Rhenna Morgan is a happily-ever-after addict—hot men, smart women, and scorching chemistry required. A triple-A personality with a thing for lists and an almost frightening iPhone cover collection, Rhenna's a mom to two beautiful little girls, and married to an extremely patient husband who's mastered the art of hiding the exasperated eye roll.

When she's not neck deep in the realm of Eden, or living large in one of her contemporary stories, she's probably driving with the top down and the music up loud, plotting her next hero and heroine's adventure. Though, trolling online for man-candy inspiration on Pinterest comes in a close second.

She'd love to share her antics and bizarre since of humor with you and get to know you a little better in the process. Check out her website at www.rhennamorgan.com for all her social media links, and signup for her newsletter for snippets, upcoming releases, and general author news. If you enjoyed *What Janie Wants*, she hopes you'll share the love with a review on Goodreads, Amazon, or your favorite online bookstore.